The **S**torm's **C**rossing

The **S**torm's **C**rossing

by Reanne S. Singer

DEACONESS
PRESS

Minneapolis

The Storm's Crossing © 1993 by Reanne S. Singer.

Published by Deaconess Press (a service of Fairview Riverside Medical Center, a division of Fairview Hospital and Healthcare Services), 2450 Riverside Avenue South, Minneapolis, MN 55454.

Cover illustration and dustjacket design by Nathan Y. Jarvis.

First Printing: June, 1993

Printed in the United States of America

97 96 95 94 93   7 6 5 4 3 2 1

Publishers's Note: Deaconess Press publishes books and other materials related to the subjects of physical health, mental health, and chemical dependency. Its publications, including *The Storm's Crossing,* do not necessarily reflect the philosophy of Fairview Hospital and Healthcare Services or their treatment programs.

Library of Congress Cataloging-in-Publication Data
Singer, Reanne S. (Reanne Sue), 1952–
     The storm's crossing / by Reanne S. Singer.
          p.   cm.
     Summary: Twelve-year-old Maggie, suffering sexual abuse from her father, struggles to deal with the problem and to begin the healing process.
     ISBN 0-925190-62-4 (hard cover)
     [1. Child molesting—Fiction. 2. Incest—Fiction. 3. Fathers and daughters—Fiction.]   I. Title.
     PZ7.S61727St   1993
     [Fic] — dc20   93-326

❖

To my parents
Who taught me to be my best;
To my children
Who teach me daily about living, loving, and dreaming;
And to the many survivors of incest and abuse
Whose struggles demanded that I write this book.

❖

It is with profound love and gratitude that I acknowledge the help and support of the following people. Cheryl Baldwin, Laurie Barringer, Joyce Kyler, and Leslie Singer provided invaluable editorial feedback. Bruce Englar, Jan Magson, Doug Maletz, Nancy Maletz, Stacy Nicholson, Barbara Singer, Herold Singer, and Allison Singer-Schwartz encouraged me to pursue writing and the publication of this manuscript, even when it was difficult. Jay Johnson, Lorrie Oswald, and Ed Wedman at Deaconess Press believed in me and my work. To all of you, and my other friends who supported me in this endeavor, I appreciate your words of encouragement and your belief in me as a writer. ❖

Chapter One

Wind blew through the branches of the sycamore tree outside Maggie's window. Maggie lay awake in bed, listening to the rustling of the dry autumn leaves and the scratching of the spindly branches against her window. The night was dark, only slightly illuminated by a sliver of moon. Shadows played on her walls, forming eerie images that gave Maggie chills. Maggie hugged her teddy bear, Willie, closer and pulled the covers more tightly around them both.

Looking around the room Maggie could barely see the outlines of the dolls and toys on the shelf above her desk. The soft black and white penguin from Aunt Joanne, Mom's sister, leaned slightly to one side. Next to it was the spotted dog Mom gave Maggie one Christmas years ago. Beside the dog was a grown-up looking doll dressed in a frilly outfit. Dad had given the doll to Maggie almost three years ago for her ninth birthday. Nine seemed like a very long time ago, thought Maggie. Now, she was almost twelve.

The most treasured of all of her toys was Willie. Grandpa had given her the teddy bear for her third birthday, and Maggie quickly took him along on games of hide-and-seek and countless tea parties. Willie soon lost a button from his shirt and his soft fur became worn from being hugged tight so often. One ear sagged slightly because Maggie would fall asleep while bending the bear's ear back and forth. Only Willie had the honor of snuggling under the covers every night with Maggie.

As she lay awake in bed, Maggie listened to the sounds in the house. Across the hall she heard her eight-and-a-half-year-old sister, Katie, turning restlessly in her bed. Their dog, Nelson, padded about the house for a few minutes, then finally settled down with a loud groan somewhere in the living room, probably near the big picture window. The television was on in the family room. Maggie could make out the voices of her parents, mixing with the TV and the other sounds in the house. The noises were reassuring to Maggie. They lulled and gently rocked her toward sleep. Maggie's heavy eyelids began to close, but she struggled to keep them open, convinced she needed to stay awake. Maggie knew she would be afraid when the noises stopped.

Maggie remembered a time when she used to fall asleep more easily. She would lay in bed feeling snug and warm and close her eyes, gently drifting off to sleep. Mom and Dad would have come to say their special good nights and tuck her in. Mom would say, "I love you more than the mountains, rivers, trees, and sky" and would bend over and kiss her softly. Dad would come in and give her a hug and kiss and tell her, "You'll always be my special little girl, my Sugar Plum Princess." Then she would snuggle under her blankets, holding onto Willie, and fall asleep. But that was a long time ago. Things were different now. Now it was frightening to fall asleep.

Maggie heard her mother's slow and labored footsteps come up the stairs and then fade down the hallway. A few minutes later, the water in the bathroom was turned on for a short time. Then Maggie again heard footsteps followed by the squeaking of mattress springs as her mother tried to get comfortable in bed. This had become a familiar sound ever since Mom's back problems and surgery three years ago. Maggie heard the same squeaking during the daytime, too, since Mom spent so much time resting in bed.

Maggie listened carefully for more sounds. Outside an owl hooted, startling Maggie, its voice echoing through the night. Her body stiffened and she lay rigid under the covers. Maggie was sure she hadn't heard her father's footsteps yet. He must have stayed downstairs for awhile longer. Maggie tried to stay awake and listen but she soon fell asleep.

Maggie woke with a start to the sound of Dad coming up the stairs. His steps were heavier and faster than Mom's. The footsteps got louder as Dad came down the hall. Maggie heard him pause ouside her room. She held her breath. Then Dad slowly walked down to the other end of the hall. Maggie did not hear any more sounds. She slowly fell into an uneasy sleep.

Maggie woke up the next morning and tried to remember about last night. She could remember cuddling with Willie. She could remember lying awake in bed, afraid. She was surprised that she slept all night without being disturbed.

Out her window, Maggie could see a morning sky with clouds that looked like huge billowing sails breaking the cold blueness. The yellow-gold leaves on the cottonwood tree outside her window moved back and forth in the wind. Maggie listened for noises in the house. It seemed quiet and hushed as though everyone else was still asleep. Maggie rummaged through her drawers and decided to wear her purple sweat pants and a pink T-shirt to school. She dressed, brushed her shoulder length chestnut hair, and quietly went downstairs. The polished wooden stairs were slippery under her stockinged feet. Maggie ran her hand down the wooden bannister. The rail was cold and smooth to her touch. It glistened in the morning light.

When Mom had hurt her back, Maggie had taken over more and more of the chores around the house. Breakfast was one that she had been doing for a long time. Mom kept telling her she could make breakfast herself now that she was feeling better, but Maggie was used to the new routine.

Maggie walked into the kitchen. Sun was coming in through the window. Maggie poured water into the coffee maker and measured out just the right amount of coffee, like Dad had taught her. She turned the switch to "on" and then got out the eggs and bread for breakfast. When Mom had her accident, Dad drew up a menu which Maggie was to follow. Eggs and toast were for Mondays, oatmeal on Tuesdays, cold cereal and sliced oranges on Wednesday, and so on through Friday. Saturdays and Sundays Dad usually took over cooking breakfast. Maggie used to enjoy helping him in the kitchen. Those were special times that they spent together, times when she did not want to share Dad with Katie. But now even those special times in the kitchen with Dad had become uncomfortable. Maggie did not like being alone with him anymore.

All by herself in the kitchen, Maggie started to think about the kinds of touching that she and Dad did. The hugs he used to give her when she was little had been comfortable. She used to like to sit on his lap and listen to stories. Then the hugs changed. They became longer and stronger. Sometimes they even hurt. Dad's kisses had changed, too. He used to give Maggie short kisses. Those too, had become stronger and harder. Maggie wished that the kisses and hugs would stop.

Maggie's thoughts were interrupted by footsteps. She could hear people walking around upstairs. Someone was in the bathroom, opening and closing a drawer and then running the water.

"Dad, do you know where my blue jean skirt is?" Katie yelled. "I can't find it."

Instead of Dad answering, Mom called, "It's still in the laundry. Find something else to wear today, Katie."

"Aw, Mom, I was counting on wearing that," Katie whined.

"We don't have time for this, Katie," Dad interrupted. "Get going and find something else to wear."

Maggie guessed that it was time to heat up the pan and start the eggs. She got out the medium sized pan and then pulled down the blue plastic bowl from the cupboard above the sink to break the eggs into.

Maggie heard Dad walking down the stairs and through the hallway toward the kitchen. She found herself stiffening. Then her tension eased as she heard Katie scurrying down the stairs after him. Dad walked in. He was dressed in a blue suit, and the tie he wore was the yellow and blue striped one that Maggie had picked out for his birthday. Maggie looked up at her father, thinking how handsome he was. His light brown hair was streaked with blonde. In the summer, the sun bleached it even lighter. Katie's hair was like this, too. Everyone said it looked like sunshine was playing through it. Maggie's hair was much darker, with a reddish tint, more like Mom's. Maggie had always wanted hair like Katie and Dad's. What she did have like Dad was freckles across her nose. That used to be fun. But now that she was growing up, she was not so sure if she liked them. Both Mom and Dad were tall and slender. People said that it seemed like Katie and Maggie would both be tall like their parents.

Maggie turned back to mixing the eggs. "Good morning, Sugar Plum," said Dad as he came over and gave her a kiss on the cheek and a hug. The hug lasted just a little too long.

Continuing to mix the eggs, Maggie mumbled, "Good morning."

Just then, Katie came into the kitchen. "Hey, Katie, how about bringing the paper in for me?" asked Dad. "It's still out front."

Katie turned to retrieve the paper. Maggie's father walked past Maggie, gently patting her on the bottom, and poured himself a cup of coffee. Then he walked over to the table and sat down.

Katie brought the newspaper in to Dad and began talking about school and friends. "You should have seen the lizard Jimmy brought in to class yesterday. It was really neat. We got to touch it. Its skin was smooth but not slimy like I thought it would be. I want to take Nelson to school. I'll bet the kids would like seeing him."

Maggie looked up. "Katie, that's a dumb idea. Nelson wouldn't like school. He would want to lick everyone and you'd have to tell him no and make him sit. I'm sure your teacher wouldn't want you to bring that big of a sharing thing to school."

Maggie did not want Katie to take Nelson to school. Nelson was her special friend and she did not want Katie dragging him around at school. He was a huge, furry dog, the size and shape of an English sheep dog, but with the peach coloring of a golden retriever. Standing on his hind legs, he could put his front paws on Dad's shoulders. Grandpa had brought Nelson the Christmas when Maggie was five years old. Nelson was just a shaggy peach-colored puppy then. He had grown and grown, and Mom and Dad used to joke that he might never stop growing. Nelson had quickly become Maggie's confidante. He listened well and was always available to play with or snuggle up against.

Katie kept on talking, ignoring Maggie's objection. Dad looked up from his paper. "Maggie's right, Katie. Nelson would be hard to handle at school. Let's see if we can't figure out something else for you to take to share."

Katie started to protest, but Dad answered her more strongly now. "Katie, that's it. I do not want to go round on this! Now go tell your mother breakfast is almost ready."

Katie knew by the sound of Dad's voice that she better not argue, or she'd lose the privilege of playing with Jenny after school. Jenny lived around the corner. Katie and she were working on building a hideout. So Katie turned away, glaring at Maggie as their eyes met. Then she stomped out of the room and went to the bottom of the stairs to call her mother.

Maggie brought the eggs and toast to the table and turned back to get the milk. Dad always insisted that Katie and Maggie drink at least one glass of milk with each meal. Dad was very concerned that they eat the right kinds of foods to stay strong and healthy, but not so much that they would get fat. He said he always wanted Katie and Maggie to be his perfect and beautiful little girls.

Maggie heard Mom coming down the stairs. She could tell when it was her mother. Mom still walked a little more slowly and carefully than the rest of the family. Ever since she had fallen that day in the rain, twisting her back, things had changed.

Mom could not do the things she had done before, the housework and cooking, taking Maggie and Katie to the park, or going for bike rides with the whole family. It seemed like that was when Dad had changed, too. First he was real worried about Mom. Then Dad became tired from all the extra work he did around the house. He started doing the laundry, shopping, and cooking. On top of that, Dad would get up in the middle of the night to get Mom her medicine for the pain. Later, Dad had taken Maggie and Katie aside and explained to them that he needed their help in taking care of things around the house. He had put his arm around Maggie and told her that since she was the oldest, she would need to be responsible for warming dinner up in the oven. Katie had only been five and a half then. Maggie, who was almost nine, had felt important and special. Dad had said he trusted her and knew that she could handle things around the house. Mom would be resting in bed after coming home from the hospital and would help if there was an emergency, but Maggie was really the one in charge. Katie and Maggie both knew they should not bother Mom unless they really had to.

Maggie did such a good job putting dinner in the oven that after awhile Dad started setting food aside on a shelf in the refrigerator for Maggie to do more of the dinner preparation—following his instructions, of course. Maggie had also taken over making sure Katie was all right in the afternoon. After school, she would meet Katie at her classroom and walk home with her, carefully holding Katie's hand in hers. Maggie would stop at each corner and check for cars before crossing the few streets on the way home. Once home, Maggie and Katie would quietly go upstairs to see Mom. If she was awake, they would gently sit down on the bed and tell her about their day. Then Maggie would take Katie downstairs, fix her a snack, and color or play a game with her. Later, Katie would watch cartoons upstairs with Mom or read a story with her, while Maggie set the table for dinner and warmed up the food. Mom and Dad were both very proud of Maggie. They said that she was being very responsible.

Sometimes on the way home from school, Maggie and Katie would stop in at Mr. Larsen's store and pick up some milk or eggs, things that Dad said they needed at home. At first Mr. Larsen would write down how much money they had spent and then get it from Dad another time. Then Dad said he thought that Maggie could handle carrying some money to school for the groceries so she could pay Mr. Larsen right when she bought the food. That had felt great! She felt so grown-up when Dad thought she was doing a good job.

Despite Maggie's help around the house, her father still looked tired. Maggie had started to worry about him. It seemed like he was not smiling as much as he used to. He also did not have the energy to play with Maggie and Katie the way he did before Mom got hurt. It used to be that he would come home in the evening and be so excited to hear about Maggie's day at school. Then he would want to play cards or a board game in the evening with the girls. On weekends there were always family outings—bike rides to the park, picnics, and trips to the zoo or the lake. But since Mom got hurt, there were always things that had to be tended to at home. Maggie was sad and missed the other times. She also did not like seeing Dad's face looking worried and tense. So Maggie started to help more and more around the house.

Soon Maggie felt like she could handle most things around the house without even asking for Dad's assistance or direction. After awhile, Dad stopped looking quite so worn out. It really seemed like Maggie was helping him feel better by taking over more of the things that needed doing in the house. The only one who did not seem to like Maggie taking all of this responsibility was Katie. She would argue when Maggie told her to do something, complaining that Maggie thought she was in charge of everything and everybody. Katie only wanted to hear from Mom and Dad what to do, not from Maggie. Maggie guessed it was because Katie was so little. But Maggie knew she had to be in charge.

"Maggie, aren't you going to come sit down with us and eat?" Mom's question interrupted Maggie's thoughts.

"Uh, yeah, Mom. I'm coming."

"Sweetie, I talk to you lately and it almost seems as if you're off somewhere else. Are you feeling OK?"

Maggie walked to the table and Mom reached over to feel her forehead. Turning to Maggie's father, Mom said, "She looks tired, doesn't she, Jim? Did you sleep all right last night, Maggie?"

Maggie nodded and mumbled that she was fine.

Mom continued, "Is anything going on at school that's bothering you?"

"No, Mom," Maggie answered, forcing a smile. "Everything is fine. I guess I was just thinking." Maggie began to pick at her eggs and took a bite of toast.

Dad reached over and rubbed Maggie's arm. He smiled reassuringly at his wife and said, "She's OK, Linda. You know how kids are. Sometimes they can be right here but their heads are a million miles away."

Dad laughed and Mom smiled back at him. She glanced once more at Maggie with concern, but now Katie was humming and clicking her fork against her glass.

"Katie, put down the fork and drink your milk," Dad said. "We're not here for band practice. Look how nicely your sister sits at the table. That's how I want you to behave."

Katie started to argue, "You always like the way Maggie acts. All I was doing was having fun..."

"Katie," Dad interrupted sternly, "that's enough. Eat your breakfast and then you need to get to school."

Katie was quiet, but when Dad went back to eating his breakfast, she managed to quickly glare at Maggie, squinting her eyes in anger. Breakfast was finished in silence. Five minutes later, Maggie and Katie were carrying their dishes over to the sink. Maggie started to rinse the dishes and load them into the dishwasher. Mom came up behind her. "Maggie, I can do those. Why don't you go finish getting ready for school?"

"I can do these, Mom. I don't mind."

Her mother put a gentle hand on Maggie's shoulder, nudging her over to the side of the sink. "Maggie, go ahead. I can take care of these." Mom gave Maggie a concerned smile.

Maggie left the kitchen and headed upstairs to get her books and jacket. On the way back down she could see Dad in the hallway. He looked up and flashed Maggie one of his charming smiles. Maggie thought to herself that maybe everything would really be all right. Dad was happy and maybe she was making more out of things than was necessary. Maggie came down the rest of the steps.

Dad looked at her, smiled again, and said, "Hey, Sugar Plum, let me see one of your terrific smiles." He gave her a hug and patted her on the bottom again. "Guess we better get going. I'll drop you and Katie off at school." He did not seem to notice that Maggie gave only a brief, strained smile.

Maggie hesitated a moment. "I think I'd like to walk today. I'll see you later."

Dad stopped short, confused, for Maggie had already turned and was off toward the kitchen yelling, "Katie, let's go. I'm walking today. C'mon if you're going with me."

Maggie grabbed the lunch bags and abruptly headed for the front door without waiting for a reply from Katie. Mom looked up from the dishes and moved to give Maggie a kiss good-bye, but she was out of reach already.

Instead Mom just called, "Have a good day, Maggie. I'll see you later." She brushed Katie's cheek with a quick good-bye kiss and sent her hurrying off to catch up with Maggie.

Katie ran after her sister calling, "Hey, wait up. What's the big hurry? We have plenty of time to get to school."

Maggie wasn't waiting. Katie would have to move quickly to catch up with her. Maggie had no intention of waiting around this morning.

Dad now called into the kitchen, "Bye, Linda. I'll see you tonight. Can you pick the girls up from ballet after work? It's our turn to drive and I have a meeting today."

Mom came into the front hall. "Yes, Jim, I'll get the girls." She moved closer to kiss him good-bye. He quickly kissed her on the forehead and turned to leave. Maggie's mother asked, "Is there anything special you'd like for dinner?"

Walking out the door, he answered without turning to look at her. "It doesn't matter. Anything is fine."

Maggie's mother stood at the doorway watching him. She thought to herself how different things used to be between them. He had been affectionate and involved with her life. They used to talk about Katie and Maggie. Everything the girls did had seemed so important and exciting to them. But over the past few years he had become more distant. It seemed to her as if he put most of his energy into work and the girls. Not much seemed to be left for her. He was always too busy or too tired to talk about much. Maggie's mother sighed as she went to finish in the kitchen and then got ready to leave for work. ❖

Chapter Two

Katie ran to catch up with Maggie. The two girls walked toward school in silence. Jenny, Katie's friend, came around the corner and joined the two sisters. Katie and Jenny were busy talking together about a mural they were working on in class. Maggie remained quiet, not even noticing they were there. They walked the five blocks to Lark Street Elementary School. At the gate, a couple of girls from Maggie's class waved to her, but Maggie did not see them.

Katie waved to them and poking Maggie gently in the side said, "Maggie, what's with you? Sarah and Lisa just said hi and you didn't even answer them."

Maggie looked embarrassed. "Oh, I guess I was just busy thinking about something." Then she quickly added, "I'll see you after school." Surprising herself, she reached over and gently squeezed Katie's hand. Maggie turned and walked off toward her classroom which was at the far end of the school.

Jenny looked at Maggie and then asked Katie, "What's with your sister? She sure has been spacey lately."

Katie shrugged. "I don't know. She has been acting a little strange. But she'll be all right. Maggie's always OK."

Maggie walked into the upper grade building and down the musty hallway. She liked the way the school smelled. The air still had a little staleness to it mixed in with the cool, fresh autumn air drifting in from outside. The plain off-white stucco walls formed a cocoon of predictability and security around her.

Maggie enjoyed school. Learning was easy and more importantly, Maggie always knew what to expect at school. There was a schedule of the day's activities posted on the board and Ms. Evans, Maggie's teacher, followed it most of the time.

Maggie thought about all the people who had walked down this hallway. She knew that older kids on her block had gone to school here and had even been in her classroom. Maggie knew Tina Mason, one of Mom's friends, who had grown up in Bayview and gone to Lark Street School. Mom said the town had not changed very much in the last thirty years. It was a little bit bigger but the tree-lined streets were much the same as they had been when Mom was a girl of Maggie's age. Many of the shops downtown had been there for ages, and the old Victorian houses near downtown still stood at proud attention on the hill overlooking a quiet bay of the Pacific Ocean, like old guards supervising what went on in town. One of Maggie's favorite old streets was Pacific Road, a few blocks away from her home. It was lined with huge jacaranda trees that formed a dark green canopy. In the spring and summer the jacarandas were covered with lavender flowers.

The bell rang reminding Maggie that it was time to go to class. Walking into the room with the other kids, Maggie saw Ms. Evans standing a few feet in from the doorway. Ms. Evans was smiling and greeting everyone. Maggie liked the way the morning sunshine bounced off Ms. Evans' gray hair. It made it sparkle like silver. Maggie walked across the room, hung her jacket on one of the hooks against the wall, and put her lunch on the shelf. At her seat, she began to unpack her books and homework, getting ready for the school day to begin.

Ms. Evans went up to the front of the room and explained what they would be doing in class today. Maggie liked Ms. Evans' smile and the way her voice sounded. Her voice was low and comforting, filled with a relaxed rhythm. When she smiled, the wrinkles and creases in her face deepened into intricate designs. Ms. Evans really seemed to be interested in sharing with her students and listening to what they had to say. Maggie noticed that Ms. Evans always looked at her when she was talking in class. She did not seem to be in a rush to go off and do other things, the way some grown-ups were. And Ms. Evans taught them all sorts of things about science. They studied botany and zoology, and made things out of papier maché and paint to go along with what they studied in books.

Even though Ms. Evans was a good teacher and made the things they studied more fun, Maggie had problems concentrating lately. She thought how easy it used to be, listening to what the teacher had to say. But sometimes she would sit at her desk and stare out the window and miss what was being said. Ms. Evans did not get upset with her though. She would just gently remind Maggie to pay attention.

The morning went by with the class doing math and then spending time studying about different kinds of fossils. During the recess break, Maggie sat under a tree and watched some kids playing ball out on the blacktop. Sarah and a few of the girls were sitting on the lawn nearby. When they motioned for her to join them, Maggie smiled faintly and shook her head no. Sarah walked over to Maggie.

"Maggie," she said, "why don't you come over with us?"

Maggie shook her head again. "Thanks," she answered, "but I think I'll just sit here for a little while. I'll see you later, OK?"

Sarah started to invite Maggie over again but Maggie cut her off. "I'm OK, Sarah. I just feel like being by myself for awhile. I've got some things I need to figure out. I'll come over with you guys later or at lunchtime."

Sarah nodded and walked back over to the other girls. She was worried about Maggie. Sarah lived up the street from her and the two girls were best friends. Maggie was becoming quieter and seemed to be thinking a lot about something important. Sarah hoped that Maggie would snap out of it soon. She used to be much more fun. Sarah wanted to help but she didn't know what to do or say to make things better for her friend.

A few minutes later, the bell rang to go back to class. Maggie spent the rest of the morning reading an assigned story in her literature book and then looking through some of Ms. Evans' books to decide on a topic for her science project.

The rest of the morning went by very quickly and soon it was time for lunch. Maggie went out onto the lawn and sat down with Sarah, Lisa, and Emily. Lisa and Emily were also in Ms. Evans' class. Eating her lunch, Maggie listened as the other girls talked about the assembly that would be held at school next week. They had permission slips to take home to allow them to attend.

Maggie wondered if Mom and Dad would let her attend the presentation. Last year there was a film and discussion about puberty and body changes. Mom and Dad had argued a great deal over that. Maggie had brought home the announcement and permission slip. Mom had seen it first and said that of course Maggie could attend. Mom thought all kids needed to hear about the changes that would be going on in their bodies.

Then Dad had seen the slip and started to chuckle. He told Maggie that whatever she needed to know, she could ask him. He told Maggie's mother they should take care of teaching the girls about their bodies at home—it just wasn't something that should be taught at school. When Mom disagreed Dad raised his voice and his smile changed into a tight, straight line cutting across his face. His eyes changed too, turning cold and distant. Maggie had felt like disappearing. She was uncomfortable when her parents argued. Usually that meant there would not be much talking between them for the next few days. Dad would be quiet and sullen. Mom would occupy herself with housework and the girls. After a few days, the family would get back to normal, but those few days were uncomfortable. Maggie had felt guilty, blaming herself for causing this fight.

The next morning Maggie had been surprised when Dad came into her room and told her she could go to the presentation. He said it was easy for him to forget that she was growing up and there was really no harm in hearing what they had to say at school. The stone-like expression on his face and the coldness in his eyes contradicted his words. Maggie felt uneasy. She asked if he was sure it was all right. Dad hurriedly said it was fine and left for work.

Maggie thought that since Dad had said yes to the film last year, he might also give his approval for the assembly coming up. Discomfort gnawed inside her stomach, though. Maggie just did not want to be the cause of any more scenes at home.

The bell rang, and lunchtime was over. The afternoon passed by, and soon it was time to go home. Maggie and Sarah met up with Katie and Jenny. Together they walked several blocks from school to Jill Everett's dance studio where they took lessons twice a week. Jenny and Katie were in the younger class. Maggie and Sarah had moved up to the more advanced level last year. This group did both ballet and jazz. Maggie enjoyed the classes. Dance came easily to her. Dad said she was very graceful, just like a prima ballerina.

The girls went into the back room of the studio. They changed into their tights and leotards and put their school clothes and books into lockers. Then Maggie and Sarah went upstairs to their class. They walked across the room to the barre to join the half dozen other students who had already begun their stretching exercises.

A few minutes later, Jill, their instructor, came into the room. She and the class practiced a dance they had started working on last week. The moves were difficult but Maggie and Sarah watched intently as Jill demonstrated the steps. She took them through the first half of the dance, stopping the music and repeating the movements whenever the students seemed confused. Maggie liked Jill and enjoyed the way she taught. The time went by quickly and the hour and a half class was soon over.

The girls went downstairs to the dressing room and threw clothes on over their leotards. Katie and Jenny were already changed and waiting for them. They grabbed their school things and went outside. Maggie's mother was parked at the curb in their green station wagon. Katie ran over to the car and hopped in front next to her mom. Maggie climbed in back with Sarah following after her. Jenny scooted in next to Katie up in front.

"Well, how did everyone's day go today?" asked Mom as she headed for home.

Katie quickly began talking about her day, with Jenny chiming in. It seemed to Maggie that Katie rambled on and on, not paying much attention to what anyone else said. Katie usually talked this way when she was happy. Maggie smiled to herself, thinking how carefully you had to listen to understand what Katie was talking about. Katie changed subjects quickly without any warning.

"It was a great day, Mom. We smeared them, right Jen?" Katie was telling Mom about the kickball game between her class and the other third graders. Katie briefly looked over at her friend.

"Yeah, she's right, Mrs. Davis. We beat them 6–2."

Katie's pace quickened. "And, Mom, we did this neat art project today. You take these crayons and cover your whole paper with them. Then you cover all that with black. Then, you know what? You draw a picture with a paper clip and it turns out in rainbow colors."

Mom laughed. "Wait a minute, Katie. Slow down. I don't understand."

"It's easy, Mom. First you put all the colors on, just like I said. Then when the black crayon is on it covers the colors and then you use a paper clip to scrape away parts of the black and the colors show through—get it?" Not waiting for an answer, Katie continued. "Our book reports are due next week and for science we started a unit on spiders."

"Sounds like a busy day, Katie."

"Yeah, it was, Mom," Katie answered.

Mom looked in the rearview mirror. "Maggie, Sarah, was school all right today? What did you two do?"

"It was fine, Mrs. Davis," said Sarah. "We did science in the morning and next week..."

Maggie cut Sarah off abruptly. She was concerned that Sarah would bring up the presentation. Maggie was not quite ready to approach that subject. "Mom," she said, suddenly animated, "we listened to a great book today in class. Ms. Evans read the beginning of it to us today after lunch. It's all about two kids who can fly to different planets and go off to explore."

"Sounds interesting," said Mom.

"Yeah," said Sarah. "It really is neat. They can fly around and then come back to Earth whenever they're ready." Sarah seemed to have forgotten what she had started to say. Maggie felt relieved.

Maggie continued talking about other activities at school. "The science lesson today was great, Mom. We studied about fossils and tomorrow we get to make our own out of clay."

"Ms. Evans sounds like a good teacher," said Mom. "You certainly are learning a great deal in her class this year."

They dropped Jenny off at her house, around the block from Maggie and Katie's. Jenny dashed out of the car yelling a quick thanks over her shoulder and, "Talk to you later, Katie. See you at school."

Mom drove the car around the corner toward home. The street lights were on, shining down on the quiet street. Well-kept lawns lined the sidewalks. Short walkways led from the driveways up to the front doors of houses. Small touches like brightly colored flowers and stone walkways made each house different from the other. Sarah's front yard was filled with impatiens in shades of pink and purple and a soft blanket of white and lavender sweet alyssum. Mom pulled the car over to the curb and Sarah opened the car door.

"Thanks, Mrs. Davis. I'll see you tomorrow, Maggie. Don't forget to have that slip signed. Bye, Katie," Sarah called as she hopped out and swung the door shut. She ran up to her house, waving once more before disappearing inside.

Maggie could feel herself becoming nervous. She hoped her mother had not heard Sarah's comment about the permission slip.

"Maggie," Mom said as she pulled the car into their driveway, "what slip was Sarah talking about? Do you have something I need to see?"

"Uh, what Mom?" Maggie hesitated. "Oh, the notice from school? Yeah. Ms. Evans sent one home with us. It's not really anything important."

"Well, what is it, Maggie?" Mom asked. "If Ms. Evans sent it home, it's important enough for me to look at."

"Yeah, I guess so," said Maggie. "It's here in my backpack. It's just about this assembly we're having at school. Something about growing up and what we need to know."

Maggie reached into her blue denim backpack, pulled out the paper, and handed it over the seat to her mother. Katie had already opened the door and climbed out of the car. Maggie slipped out of the back and followed Katie up to the front porch. As Mom came up the steps, she barely glanced at the school notice. She unlocked the door and Maggie and Katie ran upstairs to put their school things away. Mom went into the kitchen, put her purse down, and read the announcement from school. It said that there would be a presentation and discussion for sixth graders. They would learn about body changes and how to tell the difference between "good touches" and "bad touches." The notice also said that students would be taught how to take care of themselves and to say no to bad touches. The program would be held one week from Friday and parents were welcome to attend.

Maggie's mom started to sign the permission slip and then hesitated, remembering her husband's reaction to last year's presentation at school. She put the paper aside on the kitchen counter, deciding to discuss it with Maggie's father when he got home from work that evening. She didn't think he would have any objections to Maggie attending, but it seemed safer to talk about it with him first. They seemed to have arguments so easily lately. She wanted to avoid any more of them.

Maggie's mom let Nelson in from the backyard. Then she went upstairs to change out of her work clothes before starting dinner. Nelson bounded up the stairs and went straight to Maggie's room. Maggie's mother could hear Maggie talking to the dog.

"Hey, Nelson," Maggie said. "How's my pal?" She bent down and hugged him, scratching him behind the ears, just the way he liked. Maggie started to do her homework and Nelson curled up beside her.

Mom stopped in at Maggie's room before going downstairs. Maggie was sitting at her desk with her back to the doorway. She had her homework in front of her but was busy staring out the window.

"Maggie," said Mom, "is everything going all right? You've been kind of quiet lately. You seem to have your mind on something."

Without looking at her mother Maggie said, "I'm fine, Mom. Maybe I'm just a little tired."

Mom walked over and tenderly touched Maggie's shoulder. Maggie noticed what a soft touch her mother had.

"Well, let's get you into bed a bit early tonight, Maggie," said her mother. "You're sure that's all it is?"

Maggie looked up into her mother's hazel eyes. "Mom, I'm fine," she said. "Really, I'm OK."

Mom gave her a soft squeeze on the shoulder and said, "I'll be downstairs getting dinner going if you need me."

"Do you need any help?" asked Maggie, already halfway out of her chair.

Maggie's mother smiled at her, thinking that she was always so responsible and ready to help, sometimes too responsible for an eleven-year-old. "No, you go ahead and get your own work done," she said.

"But I could leave this for now and..."

"I can handle dinner, Maggie," her mother said. "You know, sweetie, I'm better now and you don't have to take care of things the way you did after my accident."

"OK, Mom, if you're sure." Maggie went back to doing her homework. Soon she was gazing out the window again. She saw the gold-colored leaves on the sycamore tree just outside her window. The tree was so close she could easily reach out the window and touch a branch. Birds would occasionally flit off a branch and soar up toward the sky, later veering in an arc and lighting once again in the tree.

Maggie remembered Grandpa saying these birds were white crowned sparrows. You could tell by the black and white stripes on their heads. Grandpa knew all about birds. Maggie loved to take long walks with him at his house in the mountains. Even when Grandpa came to Bayview to visit, they would go bird-watching and he would tell Maggie the different names of the birds. He knew where they made their nests and where they migrated during the year. He even knew the different sounds the birds made. Maggie thought how wonderful it would be to be able to fly like those birds soaring free in the sky and not having to deal with the problems people had.

Maggie remembered the permission slip from school and the assembly that would follow. She suddenly felt anxious. There was a heavy knot in her stomach. She wondered how Dad would react when he found out about the assembly. He was so protective of her, treating her like she was still a little girl. He was really picky about what extra activities she participated in, who her friends were, what she read, and what movies she went to. The list seemed to go on and on. Maggie hated that. Why did he have to be in charge of everything? ❖

Chapter Three

Maggie continued to stare out the window, no longer seeing the tree or the birds. She thought back to a lunchtime last year when she was in Mr. Bellam's fifth grade class. She had been out on the playground with Sarah, Emily, and Lisa. Lisa started talking about the special film they would be seeing on puberty. The other girls had giggled a little when Lisa brought up the subject. Lisa wasn't laughing though.

"I don't know," said Lisa. "I guess it sort of scares me. You know, the whole idea of my body changing and being able to have a baby. I'm afraid it will hurt. And the bleeding every month. I think it's embarrassing." The other girls nodded in agreement.

Maggie looked around at her friends and shrugged. "Yeah, but it can't be so bad. All women go through it. My dad says it's just nature—it's normal."

"Your dad?" asked Lisa. "You talk to him about those things?"

"Sure," Maggie answered. "My dad talks to us about all that kind of stuff."

Lisa shrugged, looking uncomfortable. Then Sarah interrupted, "But what about the touching that goes with growing up, and the way you make babies? It seems sort of gross sometimes."

"It does sound kind of yucky, doesn't it?" said Lisa. "I can't imagine ever doing anything like that with any of the boys I know."

Emily teasingly poked Lisa in the ribs. "Not even with Tommy?"

"Emily, I wouldn't! You know that!" Lisa indignantly pushed Emily back.

"I know, Lisa. I'm just kidding. But sometimes it seems so romantic," said Emily, "like in the movies, I mean. You know, falling in love and all."

"Yeah," Sarah joined in, "I guess I'm just not ready for that kind of

stuff yet. I sure hope I feel more ready when I'm older. It just seems weird. Can you imagine being touched like that now?"

Maggie noticed Emily and Lisa shaking their heads no with Sarah, so she did the same thing. That was when she had started to wonder. It did not sound as if Sarah, Emily, or Lisa had ever been touched the way Maggie had. Maybe it wasn't OK when Dad came up to her room late at night when everyone else in the house was asleep. Sometimes Maggie would be asleep, too. Other times she would be awake, tossing and turning in bed, not knowing if Dad was going to come into her room, not knowing if the touching would happen again.

Now Maggie's friends were saying that they were afraid of that kind of touching. Did that mean it didn't happen to them? Not to any of them? Maybe it meant Dad loved her in a special way. That's what he had said. He had told her he loved her so much and when people love each other, touching becomes part of that love. Part of Maggie believed this. But part of her was beginning to wonder.

She was feeling chilly even though the sun was shining brightly and she had been comfortable just a few minutes ago. She could feel dampness underneath her arms. Then she heard Sarah's voice. "Maggie, are you with us? Maggie. Hey, Maggie!" Sarah moved closer to her.

Maggie looked up, startled. "What? Oh, yeah, Sarah."

Now Emily was talking. "Maggie, what's with you? You looked like you were in outer space or something."

"Yeah," said Lisa. "You don't look very good. You're real pale."

Maggie looked around at the three girls. "I'm fine," she answered. "I was just thinking about something." Changing the subject she said, "What do you guys think about the report for Mr. Bellam? Have you picked out a book to read yet?"

Lisa and Emily started talking about the books they had selected. Sarah sat watching, thinking that it was strange how preoccupied Maggie had suddenly become. When the bell rang and lunchtime was over, the four girls started walking back to Mr. Bellam's class. Lisa and Emily walked a little ahead of Sarah and Maggie. Sarah decided to talk

to Maggie about dance class. Dance was something that both Sarah and Maggie really enjoyed. It was time they shared together, something special in their friendship.

"Maggie," said Sarah, "those jumps we started working on in ballet class sure are something, aren't they?" Maggie just nodded so Sarah continued. "Jill makes them look so easy, like she's flying. But when I try them, I can't get up very high. I guess it takes a lot of work. I sure hope that someday I can do them like she does. She's so graceful."

Maggie seemed to cheer up. "How long do you think she's up in the air when she does those jumps?" asked Sarah. "It looks like forever. What's the name of those anyway? Do you remember what she called them?"

"Um...," Maggie hesitated a moment, fishing for the words. "*Grand jeté*, I think."

"That sounds right," said Sarah. "But when I see it written down I think of 'grand jet.'"

The two girls laughed as they walked down the hallway and into Mr. Bellam's room. Some of the kids were already in the classroom. Together, Maggie and Sarah walked over to their seats on the far side of the room. In Mr. Bellam's class, the students had been allowed to choose their own seats. Sarah and Maggie had chosen to sit together. Maggie liked that.

Mr. Bellam was up in front writing on the chalkboard. Maggie thought he was one of the nicest teachers in the whole school. He never yelled at the kids. He had a special system where kids in his class earned points for completed assignments. Every Friday afternoon they totalled up their points and cashed them in like money for special privileges. They could rent a game of checkers or Parchesi from Mr. Bellam to play during free time, be the first to choose what classroom chore they wanted to do the following week, or if they had a lot of points they could choose a special activity that the whole class would do for free time. On Saturdays, Mr. Bellam took a few of the students at a time on special outings. By the end of the year, everyone had a chance for an outing. They did things like hiking up to the falls at

Miller's Creek; fossil hunting; or, if it was close to Halloween, going on a hayride at the pumpkin patch. Maggie hoped she would be able to go on a trip at the same time as Sarah. It would be more fun if they went together.

Maggie sat at her desk, occasionally glancing around the room. She did not whisper with Sarah as she usually did right before class started. Maggie was still wondering if what went on at her house happened at the homes of her friends. If the way Dad touched her was different from the way other fathers behaved, then maybe both she and her father had done something wrong. Maybe people would be angry with her if they ever found out. But they couldn't find out, not unless someone told. Maggie knew she would not tell. Not ever.

Now Mr. Bellam was telling one of the corny jokes he was known for. Maggie found herself starting to smile, just slightly. "A boy rode up in an elevator and when they got to the top floor, the elevator operator said, 'Here you are, son.' The boy said, 'Don't call me son, you're not my father.' The elevator operator said, 'I brought you up, didn't I?'"

Mr. Bellam and the whole class laughed. When Mr. Bellam laughed, his round belly shook up and down and his whole face seemed to light up smiling. Maggie wasn't sure who enjoyed the jokes more, Mr. Bellam or the kids. She loved it when everyone in the class was smiling and laughing. Not like at home, Maggie thought. It didn't seem like her family laughed together as much as they used to. Mom and Dad didn't smile at each other very often, either. Maggie and Katie argued. Dad seemed to be off with his own thoughts a lot of the time.

"Preoccupied" was the word Maggie heard Mom use when Mom and Dad argued. "Preoccupied" and "distant." Dad still paid attention to her and Katie, and he often told Maggie that she was his special girl. He saved that for times when they were alone, though.

Maggie suddenly heard Mr. Bellam's voice addressing her. "Maggie," he was saying, "you'll be working with Jeremy, Sarah, Allison, John, and David on math today. I want that group sitting over here," he said pointing to the table closest to the windows. "Jeremy, you can pull out the wooden cubes to help with the calculations. Maggie,

24

would you get enough pencils, erasers, and paper for your group, please?"

Maggie nodded her head and started walking over to the shelf where the wooden cubes were kept. Jeremy stopped her. "Maggie, you're supposed to get the paper and stuff. Mr. Bellam asked me to get the cubes. Weren't you listening?"

"He told me to get the cubes, Jeremy. You don't have to boss me around." Maggie's voice was unusually harsh.

"Maggie, he didn't. He said for you to go get the paper! I'm the one getting the cubes."

"No. That's not right," Maggie snapped. "You're wrong, Jeremy. You just don't know."

Maggie felt confused. Now she wasn't sure at all what directions she had heard from Mr. Bellam. Maybe Jeremy was right.

Jeremy looked curiously at Maggie. It was not like her to get directions mixed up. And it certainly was not like her to get angry. "Maggie," Jeremy said more calmly, "it's not that important. You can go get the cubes if you want to."

Maggie stood there, embarrassed, shaking her head. "No, go ahead." She hesitated for a moment and then added, "Sorry, Jeremy. I thought he said for me to get the cubes." Her face felt warm and flushed. She hoped that nobody noticed. She didn't want Jeremy to think that she was weird. Maggie thought that Jeremy was the cutest boy in the whole class, with his freckles and shaggy red hair.

Mr. Bellam walked over to them. "Is there a problem, Maggie and Jeremy?"

Maggie did not answer. Jeremy said, "It's OK, Mr. Bellam. We worked it out."

Mr. Bellam looked over at Maggie and noticed that she was blushing. "Maggie," he said, "why don't you go get six pencils and erasers and a stack of plain paper for your group."

Maggie went off toward the rear shelves to gather the supplies. Mr. Bellam watched her for a moment, wondering what was going on. Maggie usually had no problem following directions or getting along with the other kids in class.

Maggie picked up the things she needed and brought them to the table. As she walked by Jeremy, he looked up at her. "Sorry, Jeremy," she mumbled.

"Me, too," said Jeremy. "Don't worry about it."

Maggie sat down across the table from Sarah. Sarah gave her a quizzical look and whispered, "What was all that about?"

"Nothing," Maggie whispered back. "No big deal."

Maggie spent about half an hour working in the math group. Then it was cleanup time and the students returned to their own seats. This period was followed by art. They were working with charcoal in class, doing sketches of trees and plants. Maggie usually enjoyed art time. Today, however, she was not really in the mood.

Maggie spent much of the art session struggling to draw but she mostly sat and stared out the window, thinking about home. She heard the lunchtime conversation with Lisa over and over in her head. Her stomach was hurting and her hands felt cold.

Finally she heard Mr. Bellam saying that it was time to clean up the art materials and get ready to go home. Maggie scooped up her charcoal, putting it back in the shoebox at the front of the room. She put her unfinished picture in her art cubby, planning to complete it tomorrow. She returned to her seat and tried to concentrate as Mr. Bellam gave the class their homework assignment. Then Maggie gathered up her jacket and the vocabulary list she would have to study at home. Leaving the classroom, she caught sight of Mr. Bellam smiling slightly at her. She walked out onto the playground. Sarah came running up behind her and they cut across the yard on their way to meet Katie at the school yard gate.

Sarah looked at her friend. "Maggie, is anything going on? You look kind of funny."

Maggie paused for a moment and then said, "I'm OK. My stomach's just hurting a little bit. I'll be fine."

Just then, Katie and Jenny came running to meet Sarah and Maggie. Katie was smiling and laughing with Jenny. The mild autumn breeze blew wisps of hair about their faces. Katie was flushed from running and was jubilant about her day. Bounding over to Maggie, Katie announced that she had been selected as the representative from her class for the student council.

Maggie smiled. "That's great, Katie. I bet Mom and Dad will really be proud of you." Maggie was finding it difficult to be excited but knew that this was a special honor.

Together they headed toward home. "Yeah," said Katie, "we're going to have meetings every Tuesday at lunchtime. Mr. Bellam's the teacher in charge, you know."

"I know," answered Maggie. "It's terrific, Katie." She used the words that she knew Katie would want to hear but her tone was flat.

"Maggie," Katie continued, "has anyone been chosen yet as the representative from your class?"

"No, not yet," answered Maggie. "We're deciding that tomorrow."

"Hey, Maggie, wouldn't it be fun if you were elected and then we could be on the council together?"

"I don't think I'll get it this year, Katie. It will probably be someone else's turn."

Maggie had been on the student council the year before. This made it even more special to Katie who wanted to be like her big sister.

"I don't know, Maggie," said Sarah. "The kids all really like you. You just might be the representative again."

Maggie shrugged. "I don't know. It's not all that important anyway."

Maggie just could not seem to get herself interested in being in student council again this year. Last year it had been exciting to her. Now she wondered why it suddenly seemed so unimportant. Katie left Maggie's side and walked a few paces ahead to talk with Jenny. Maggie and Sarah quietly walked the next few blocks toward home.

The girls crossed the last street on their way home. At the corner, Jenny headed around the block to her house. Two doors up from the Davis' house, Sarah turned into her own yard, waving good-bye to Maggie and Katie. She called over her shoulder, "Maggie, do you want to play this afternoon? We could ride bikes or something."

"My dad will be calling home soon to make sure we got in OK and check on us. I'll ask him if I can play and let you know," Maggie answered.

"Great," called Sarah.

Sarah walked up to her house. Her mother's car was parked in the driveway. Her mother opened the front door, smiling. Maggie watched as she gave Sarah a big hug.

Sarah's mother waved and called to the girls, "Would you like to come in for a snack?"

Katie started to nod yes but Maggie said, "No thanks, Mrs. Bloom. We better get home. Maybe we can come by later."

Sarah's mom nodded as she and Sarah turned to go inside. Katie started to protest. "Maggie, I want to go to Sarah's. Her mom said it was fine. Can't we just go for a little while?"

"Katie, you know Dad said we have to come straight home after school. And we can't go anywhere without checking with him first." Maggie's voice had taken on a tone that was a combination of Mom's and Dad's. It had Mom's matter-of-fact sound and Dad's seriousness and intensity.

"But, Maggie, it's just Sarah's house," Katie whined. "You always have to be in charge of everything!"

"That's not fair, Katie. Dad said I'm responsible for what goes on here when he and Mom are at work. We just can't go without permission. Dad will get really mad if we do that. You know that."

"I guess you're right," answered Katie, giving in to Maggie for the moment. "But I sure don't like all of Dad's rules sometimes...or yours."

As they reached the brick walkway leading up to their house, Maggie pulled out the housekey from her backpack. Maggie unlocked the door and as they walked in, she noticed the closed-up smell of the house. It was different from the the crisp, fresh air outside or the musty smell at school. The school smell was warm and secure. The smell of her house made Maggie think of a sealed box. It was odd having this smell suddenly be so unpleasant.

Maggie walked into the kitchen and read the note on the counter about what to put on for dinner. Nothing needed to be done for the next hour, so she went upstairs to change out of her school clothes.

Walking into her bedroom, she thought back to the lunchtime conversation about Lisa saying that the idea of certain kinds of touching frightened her. Did that mean Lisa had never been touched in those ways? What about Emily and Sarah? Did their fathers touch them like that? Maggie's stomach was starting to ache again and she could feel her hands becoming clammy as she thought about the way Dad touched her and... The telephone rang, startling Maggie. She heard Katie running into Mom and Dad's bedroom and then the ringing stopped.

Katie's voice carried through to her room. "Yes, Daddy. Everything's fine." There was a pause and then, "No, not too much homework tonight. Just some spelling words. Can we go outside for a little while? Sarah's Mom invited us over for a snack...or could we just go out front to play with Jenny and Sarah?" It was quiet and then Katie said, "Yeah, Maggie's in her room. Do you want me to get her?" After a minute Katie yelled, "Maggie. Daddy's on the phone. He wants to talk to you."

Maggie did not feel very eager to talk with her father. She went to her parents' room and crossed over to the night stand next to her father's side of the bed. She picked up the phone receiver.

"Hi, Dad," she said as cheerfully as possible.

"Hi, Mag," she heard him answer. "Everything all right?"

"Uh-huh," said Maggie.

"Well, how was school?"

"School was fine," Maggie responded flatly.

"Did you see the note about dinner?" asked Dad.

"Yeah, I saw it. I'll put the meat in the oven about 4:30."

"Thanks, Sugar Plum. I'll be home about 5:30. I love you."

Maggie paused and said, "I'll see you later." Then, "Dad, can Katie and I go outside for awhile to play?"

"Sure," he answered. "Just don't go too far—not off the block."

"Thanks," said Maggie. She started to hang up the phone but Dad was talking again.

"Hey, Mag, how about an 'I love you' for poor, old Dad?"

"I love you," said Maggie quietly. "I'll see you later tonight." Maggie placed the receiver down and turned to walk out of the room.

Katie eagerly followed her asking, "Did he say we could go, Maggie? Can we go over to Sarah's or can I call Jenny?"

"What?" asked Maggie absently. Then looking over at her sister, she remembered what Katie wanted. "Oh, yeah, Katie. You can call Jenny. We just have to stay close to home."

"Great," said Katie. A wide smile crossed her face. She hurried back over to the phone and dialed Jenny.

Katie finished her call and came to the doorway of Maggie's room. "Let's go, Maggie. Are you going to call Sarah?"

Maggie sighed. Everything seemed to be a chore today. "I guess so," she said. "Maybe I'll just walk up to Sarah's house and see if she wants to come outside. I don't know. Maybe I should go ahead and call Sarah before going up there."

Maggie was not feeling very enthusiastic, but maybe going out for awhile with her friend would cheer her up. Maybe she could even ask Sarah some questions to figure out if she really needed to be upset and worried about anything.

Maggie slowly walked into Mom and Dad's room and sat down on their bed. She dialed Sarah's number and her friend answered.

Maggie spoke softly into the phone. Her words seemed to come slower than usual. "Sarah, it's Maggie. My dad says it's fine to come out for awhile. Do you want to meet me out front?"

"Sure," said Sarah. She was already noticing that Maggie was upset about something. "Unless you'd rather come over to my house and hang around inside for awhile."

Maggie hesitated. She wanted to talk with Sarah without being overheard by Sarah's mother. "No, let's go outside today."

"OK," said Sarah. "I'll be right out."

Maggie went back to her room, picked up her sweatshirt and called down to Katie, "I'm going out to see Sarah. Is Jenny coming over?"

Katie already had the front door open and was ready to go outside.

"I'm going over there. We're going to skate out in front of her house."

"OK, but don't go off the block," warned Maggie.

"I know, I know, " Katie answered, slightly exasperated. There was Maggie repeating Mom and Dad's rules again.

Maggie heard Katie heading outside. Maggie slowly left the house, too, turning her face into the afternoon breeze. Sarah was just coming out of her house and she waved to Maggie.

"Hi, Maggie. Look!" Sarah held up her other hand. "My mom made these muffins today. Here's one for you. We can sit on the grass and eat them."

The two girls sat on Sarah's front lawn, quietly munching on their carrot muffins. Sarah's mom was always doing things like baking snacks for Sarah and her younger sister and brother. Sometimes Maggie wished her mom was around when she got home from school, just to give her a big hug and talk about the day.

Maggie finished the last bite of muffin and looked over at Sarah. Tentatively she said, "Sarah, what did you think about what Emily and Lisa were saying at lunch today?"

Sarah looked at Maggie questioningly. "What do you mean? What they were saying about what?"

"Oh, you know." Maggie tried to sound unconcerned. "About babies and all—how they're made and it being creepy to think about being touched like that."

"I don't know," Sarah paused for a moment. "I guess when you're older, it doesn't seem weird any more. When you like a boy in a special way, maybe it's nice to be hugged and touched. But I guess what Emily and Lisa meant is that it would be real strange to have that happen now."

Maggie could feel her hands getting sweaty again. She noticed every heartbeat in her chest. Her eyes focused on the blades of grass on Sarah's front lawn. She fingered single blades, not even noticing what she was doing.

Trying to stay calm, she asked, "Have you ever been touched by anyone? You know, touched like when people really love each other a lot?" Maggie tentatively raised her eyes to look at Sarah. Please say yes, she thought to herself. Your answer has to be yes.

"Of course not," answered Sarah emphatically. "I'm only ten, you know. It would be all right when I'm much older, but not now." Maggie was looking at Sarah very intently now. Noticing this, Sarah felt she needed to explain further to her friend. "Look," Sarah said, "it wouldn't be weird if Jeremy tried to hold your hand, right? Because you like him. Maybe when you're older, if you were in love with him, it would be OK to touch like Emily and Lisa were talking about, but not now."

Maggie nodded in agreement but persisted with her questions. She had to get more information. She had to try to understand. "But, Sarah, does that mean no one has ever touched you...your body...in special ways?"

Sarah looked bewildered. "What do you mean, Maggie? I get hugs and stuff from my folks. Or when my grandparents come over, they always want to kiss me. Sometimes they forget I'm getting older and they even want to kiss me when we're out somewhere. It's kind of embarrassing. Is that what you mean?"

Maggie was feeling more and more anxious. Her chest felt as if her heart was going to pound a hole right through it, and her head hurt with a dull ache. Was her father that different from Sarah's? Maggie waited, deciding whether to ask one more question. But she had to know.

"Sarah, what do you mean *and stuff*? What kinds of hugs and kisses do you get?"

Sarah looked at Maggie, her eyes confused. The expression on her face was very serious and intense. She finally said, "Maggie, they just hug and kiss me. Regular stuff, that's all. They hug me around the shoulders or waist and they kiss me on the face. Sometimes we wrestle and tickle. Is that what you want to know?" Sarah's eyes searched Maggie's, waiting for her to answer.

After a long moment, Maggie saw Sarah's confusion and concern. Maggie answered, "Yeah, that's all I wanted to know. Sometimes people do things different in different families. I...just sort of wanted to know how it was in your family." Now Maggie understood that things were different in Sarah's home. Very different. It did not sound as though Sarah's dad acted anything like the way Maggie's did, with his middle-of-the-night visits to her bedroom.

Now Sarah was looking at Maggie very seriously. "Well, how is it in your family?"

Maggie shrugged, trying to make light of it. She forced a smile. "It's like you said, just hugs and kisses. No big deal."

Maggie could not remember having lied to Sarah before. Sarah was her best friend, and that meant telling each other the truth. But Maggie just couldn't tell this to Sarah. She couldn't tell anyone, not until she understood more about what was happening.

"C'mon," said Maggie, changing the subject. We still have an hour to play until I have to go in. Let's get our bikes and ride." Maggie stood up on the lawn.

"OK," said Sarah, "I'll just be a minute. Mine's in the garage."

"I'll be right back," said Maggie. "I have to go get mine, too."

Maggie walked down the street toward home. Thoughts were tumbling through her head. She was glad to have a couple of minutes alone. She tried to calm herself down. She did not want Sarah to figure out how worried and frightened she was. Sarah was good at figuring out things about Maggie. Maggie would have to work hard today to keep her feelings secret from Sarah.

The girls rode up and down the street pretending their bicycles were horses. Maggie calmed down as she became distracted by their game. The pounding in her chest stopped. Only a mild ache remained in her head. She gave her pretend horse a name and they played that they were galloping up over steep hills on their mounts. Once in awhile they would stop to water their horses and rest. Neither Sarah or Maggie mentioned their earlier conversation. A couple of times that afternoon Maggie noticed Sarah looking at her strangely, but Maggie did not ask why. She did not want to talk any more about her family or Sarah's. Maggie hoped Sarah would forget all about the questions Maggie had asked. ❖

Chapter Four

Later that night at dinner, as Maggie sat at the table with Katie and her parents, Maggie said, "I have a permission slip that I need signed. I have to take it back to school tomorrow."

"Where is it, Maggie?" asked her mother.

Before Maggie could answer, her father said, "I have it, Linda. I found it laying on the kitchen counter." Turning toward Maggie he said, "Maggie, I don't know about this. I really think that we can teach you these kinds of things better at home."

"But, Dad, all the kids will be going." Maggie hadn't really thought that he would say no. It would be so embarrassing to go back to school like a little kid and have to say that her father would not allow her to attend the presentation.

Maggie's mother spoke up now. "Will someone please tell me what this is all about? What presentation?"

Maggie's dad continued to look at Maggie, ignoring his wife's questions. "Honey," he said appeasingly to Maggie, "I just think that some things are better taken care of at home. I can tell you everything you need to know. That's a better idea than listening to a stranger."

Maggie's mother interrupted again, exasperated this time. She said a little louder, "What are the two of you talking about? What presentation?"

"It's nothing, Linda," said Maggie's father. "Just a talk about growing up and body changes. Certainly nothing that Maggie needs to hear about at school. It's private and something that I'm sure I can handle with her."

"Jim," Mom said, "I think it would be fine for Maggie to go to the presentation at school. It's important. Who knows, they might have some better ways of presenting the material than we would. I'm sure they've given it a great deal of thought."

THE STORM'S CROSSING

Maggie was surprised her mother disagreed with her father. And Dad was becoming angry. Maggie could tell by the way his ears were turning a dark pink and the muscles in his mouth and cheeks were tightening, like he was clenching them. He was not accustomed to being challenged.

"Linda, it's just not all right with me. I can handle these things with the girls."

Maggie felt uncomfortable and confused. She wished she had never even brought up the subject of the assembly. She hated it when Mom and Dad argued. Most of the time, Mom just gave in to whatever Dad wanted. Lately, though, this had started to change. There was more fighting, more loud voices, and more times when Dad sulked around the house. Tonight Maggie felt especially responsible for the fighting.

Interrupting her parents, Maggie said, "Mom, Dad, it's not that important. Really! If Dad doesn't want me to go, I don't have to."

"No, Maggie, there's no reason not to go." Maggie's mom turned toward her husband. "Jim, is there any other reason that you have for Maggie not to go? She needs to do things with the other kids. I'm confused. I can't imagine why you would not want her to attend. You know you can't keep her a little girl forever. She's growing up whether you want her to or not."

Maggie's mother stared at her husband. Maggie's father cleared his throat and shifted his body awkwardly in the chair. Maggie did not understand what was going on between her parents but she decided to remain quiet. There was silence in the room. Katie picked at her food, intent on making designs on her plate.

Maggie's father broke the silence. "I guess you're right, Linda. I forget sometimes that Maggie is growing up and can handle these sorts of things." Then looking at his eldest daughter he said, "Mag, it's fine. I'll sign the slip for you. But remember, if you have any questions you can come to us with them." His mouth formed a tight smile. His eyes stared straight ahead. He rose from his chair and mumbled, "I'm going upstairs for a little bit. I have some paperwork to take care of." Maggie

35

and Katie watched quietly as their father left the room.

The two girls finished eating in silence. Mom cleared her place and started to straighten things in the kitchen. Maggie watched her mother moving around the room, her body working with short, angry movements. Even though Maggie's father had given in, the argument had been a struggle for her mother. Maggie did not understand what had just happened. One minute her parents were arguing and the next minute Dad was giving in. Her mother usually did not push as hard as she had tonight. If there was a disagreement, Mom was the one to back down within a short time. Maggie did not understand why her mother had stood her ground so firmly on this issue. She wanted to thank Mom but was not sure what to say. She also felt responsible for the tension in the house, for Mom's angry movements, and for Dad's quiet retreat.

Katie got up from the table carrying her dinner dishes to the sink. Maggie stacked the remaining dishes and carefully carried them over to the counter. Then she picked up the sponge from the sink, turned on the faucet, and ran warm water on the sponge so she could wipe off the table.

"Mom, do you want any more help?" Katie asked, hoping to be excused from cleaning up.

Without glancing up Mom said, "No, Katie. Go ahead. I'll get the dishes tonight."

Katie walked toward the kitchen door that led to the hallway. She turned to Maggie and said, "You want to play cards for awhile?"

Maggie looked at her sister and then glancing in the direction of her mother she said, "Maybe in a few minutes, Katie. I'll be in soon. Why don't you go get everything set up without me."

"Sure," answered Katie, quietly watching as her mother rubbed hard at a spot on the tile counter and then noisily moved dishes around in the sink. She felt uncomfortable but knew that now was not the time to ask any questions. Katie headed upstairs to her bedroom.

Maggie looked over at her mother. "Mom," she said quietly. "I just...well, you know. Thanks," she said awkwardly. "I did want to go with the other girls to hear the talk...but I didn't want to cause a problem. It's really OK if I don't go. I mean…if that will make you and Dad not mad anymore."

Mom looked over at her, the tight lines around her mouth softening slightly. "Oh, Maggie, everything will be all right. You don't have to take care of us. Dad and I will be just fine. He's just so stubborn and sensitive. You know how he gets. Don't worry. By tomorrow, he won't even care whether you go to the assembly or not." Mom came over close to Maggie and hugged her around the shoulder. "Look at this," Mom laughed. "You're so tall, you're up to my shoulder already. You're getting so big, so grown-up! Go on now. Katie's waiting for you." She gave Maggie a gentle shove toward the doorway.

"But I can help with the dishes first, Mom. Katie can wait."

"It's fine, Maggie. Go play with Katie. She needs some time with her big sister. The dishes won't take me long."

"But…"

"Maggie, go on now," Mom said more firmly. "I'm fine taking care of this."

Maggie left the room and went to find Katie. She thought to herself how much she loved Mom. She liked the way her hugs felt and the way she talked to her when she had time. Maggie walked up the stairs. Before turning down the hall to Katie's room, she quietly peeked to the right where the den was. She could see Dad sitting at his desk, his back to the door. She started to go in to talk to him but decided not to. It was uncomfortable to be around him when he was angry. He was so quiet and tense. Even the air around him felt heavy and filled with strain. So Maggie moved away from the den and walked back to Katie's room to play cards.

The two sisters played for about half an hour and then Maggie reminded Katie that they needed baths. Oftentimes they bathed alone. Maggie was getting so tall, it was impossible for her to stretch out in the tub if Katie was there. But tonight, Maggie wanted Katie's company. Dad usually came in to dry the girls off or to scrub their backs when they washed. Maggie decided that tonight she would ask Katie to wash her back. She did not like the idea of Dad coming into the bathroom. Maggie directed Katie to get a clean nightgown, and then she went to get her own nightgown and run the bathwater. Soon after, Mom came upstairs to check on the girls.

Seeing that Maggie had already gotten things ready for a bath, she said, "Thanks, Maggie. You're a big help. Do you need anything?"

"No, Mom," said Maggie. "We're fine. Katie's going to take her bath with me tonight."

"You sure?" asked Mom. "I thought you didn't like to take baths with your sister any more."

"No, it's fine, Mom. I asked her to."

"OK, Maggie. I'll be downstairs if you need me."

Maggie headed off toward the bathroom calling, "Katie, it's ready. The tub is full. Let's go."

Katie came down the hallway, smiling and happy for the attention from her sister. Halfway through their bath, Maggie heard her father's footsteps coming down the hall. Then she saw the door knob slowly turning. Maggie could feel a hollow pit in the bottom of her stomach. The door opened and her father was halfway through the doorway. Glancing in the mirror above the sink, he could see the reflection of his two daughters in the tub. A little surprised to find both of them there, he asked if they wanted any help. Looking up, Maggie announced that they would wash each others backs and would be just fine. Her tone of voice was short and abrupt.

Slightly taken aback, Dad said, "OK, Mag, if that's the way you want it." He turned and left the room, closing the door behind him.

After their baths, the two girls headed downstairs. Maggie stayed closer than usual to Katie. Katie went into the family room to watch television and Maggie followed after her. Nelson was settled in, dozing on the carpet. Maggie snuggled in next to him, stroking his soft fur. He was so big and cuddly that she could comfortably lay her head on his side and use him as a pillow. Nelson did not seem to mind. He raised his head for a brief moment and looked over at Maggie.

"Just me, Nelson," Maggie said as she patted him.

Nelson laid his head down and closed his eyes again. Maggie

watched the show Katie picked on TV. Tonight there was no argument over the girls wanting to watch different shows. Soon it was bedtime, and Maggie asked Mom if Nelson could sleep with her in her room. Mom hesitated but then agreed. Nelson always spent the night downstairs, but Maggie had seemed withdrawn and preoccupied. Maybe she needed the reassurance of having Nelson with her. Maggie called to him and he sleepily followed her up the stairs. From the hallway she called good night to her father who was back in the den.

He turned around from the desk and looked intently at Maggie. "Sugar Plum, I'll be in soon to kiss you good night."

"How about if I kiss you now?" asked Maggie. "Nelson's going to sleep with me tonight and I don't want you to let him out by coming into the room." Maggie walked into the den and reached over, giving her father a short kiss on the cheek.

"But, Mag, how can I go to sleep without saying good night properly to my sweetheart?" Maggie's father flashed her one of his charming smiles and squeezed her arm.

Maggie did not know what to say. She turned to leave the room. Then she heard her father's voice calling after her, "I'll be in soon, Maggie."

Walking down the hallway, Maggie felt afraid and confused. Once in her room, she shut the door so Nelson would not leave. She took Willie down from the shelf and turned out the light. She climbed into bed and told Nelson to lay down and go to sleep, pointing to the floor right next to the bed. Maggie lay under the covers holding onto Willie with one arm. She let her other arm dangle down the side of the bed so she could stroke Nelson's head. Minutes later, her father walked into the room. He came close and sat down on the bed.

"Good-night, Sugar Plum," he said, stroking Maggie's hair near her forehead. Maggie was quiet so he continued. "Got a kiss for a handsome dad?"

"Sure," said Maggie, directing her mouth toward his cheek.

Dad turned his face and kissed her on the lips. "What's all this,

Maggie? You're not shy all of a sudden, are you?" he said, laughing. "I love you, you know. It's important for people to show they love each other."

Maggie took a deep breath. "Dad," she said, "is it, well...is it OK the way we show we love each other?"

Dad looked at her seriously. "Is that what's been going on? Why would you ask that?" Dad's hand fell away from Maggie's forehead. His body stiffened slightly.

"I don't know," said Maggie. "Just some stuff the kids were saying at school."

"What kind of stuff?" asked Dad. "Did you tell them about the way we love each other?" His tone was now serious and concerned.

"No. You told me that's our secret. It's just that it sounds like their dads don't treat them the same way you treat me. And I just sort of wondered why. Does that mean there's something wrong with our secret times?"

Dad answered strongly and insistently. "Of course there's nothing wrong, Mag. It's just that most fathers don't have as much time with their daughters or as much closeness. We have something special. Remember? I told you that. But not everyone would understand. So you mustn't ever tell anyone about it. Besides, it's our secret and it wouldn't be as special if other people knew about it."

Maggie thought what Dad was saying made sense, but then why was there still that uneasy feeling in her stomach? She wanted to tell her father that she didn't want their secret any longer. But what if he stopped loving her then? She really wanted to be his little girl and to have him be proud of her and love her. Maybe if Nelson slept with her, Dad would not come into her room late at night. Maybe Maggie would not even have to say the words to ask him to stop.

Trying to please her father, she smiled and said, "Good-night, Dad. I love you."

"I love you too, Sugar Plum." Then he kissed her directly on the lips and left the room.

Maggie got up out of bed and closed the bedroom door. She

climbed back into bed but it was difficult to relax. Maggie finally fell asleep, her hand still dangling down into Nelson's warm fur. She awakened much later to her father sitting next to her on the bed. She could feel his hands pulling the covers down. Maggie started to tremble.

Pushing away his hand she mumbled, "No, Dad. I don't want to."

Maggie's father did not seem to hear her. As he touched her, she turned her head away, feeling powerless. He finally left the room. Maggie lay in bed crying softly to herself. Nelson was still in the room. He had moved over to the far wall. Maggie called him over to her and reached out to him for comfort. She fell asleep once again with her hand up against him.

During the night, Maggie dreamed she was being chased. She could not see the face of whatever was chasing her. All she knew was that it was some sort of creature, hairy and very large. Maggie was running away from it, down a dirt road toward the hills. She was trying to figure out a way to fool the creature, to get away from it. Up ahead, the road came to a dead end and the ground became rocky and difficult to run on. Looking back over her shoulder, Maggie saw that the creature was closer, its arms outstretched toward her.

Maggie woke up suddenly from the dream. Her heart was pounding strongly against her chest. Her hair was plastered against her scalp in damp clusters. For a moment Maggie was confused about where she was. Then she looked down and saw Nelson asleep next to her bed. She realized she was at home in her own bed and that she had been dreaming. She lay back down and stared up at the ceiling, afraid to close her eyes because she thought the nightmare might return. She dozed off much later and awoke to muted sunlight filtering into her room through the November clouds. ❖

Chapter Five

During the next few days at school, Maggie was quiet and kept to herself. She tried to pretend that everything was fine. Sarah looked at her throughout the day, wondering what was going on, but Maggie seemed to be somewhere far away. Sarah decided not to ask Maggie what was wrong.

The second morning, as the class was going out for recess, Maggie was the last one to clean up her work area and leave the room. As she was walking toward the door, Mr. Bellam stopped her. "Maggie, is there anything you would like to talk about or ask me?" His voice was soft and concerned.

Maggie glanced up at him, her eyes startled and frightened. She shook her head no and hurried to catch up with her friends out on the playground.

Mr. Bellam stood in the classroom doorway, watching Maggie walk away, concerned about the changes in her but not sure what more to do. Outside, Maggie watched the kickball game and noticed some of her friends swinging across the monkey bars. That was all she did—watch. She did not feel like playing today. After a few minutes, Sarah and Lisa waved and motioned for her to join them in their hopscotch game. Maggie smiled slightly and shook her head no. The girls went back to playing. Maggie continued to watch. A few minutes later the bell rang and it was time to return to class.

At lunchtime, Maggie joined Sarah, Lisa, and Emily on the grass. She said very little, mainly listening to their conversation and thinking about home, about Dad, and about herself.

Then on Friday came the talk on body changes. Students from the upper grade classrooms went into the auditorium and watched a movie about changes that happen to boys and girls when they reach puberty. As the film ended and the lights came on in the auditorium, a man and woman, guest speakers, talked in more detail about growing up and answered the students' questions. There was much whispering among the students and squeaking sounds as boys and girls shifted around in their seats.

From where she stood on the stage, the woman smiled at the students. "I hear lots of noise in here." There was a sudden increase of talking and then it quieted down. "The noise and whispering is fine, you know. Most boys and girls react like that when we start to talk with them about their bodies. But even though it's uncomfortable some-times to talk about these changes, it's still very important that you know what to expect with your bodies."

The man continued. "One of the most important things for you to learn here today is to ask questions about your bodies. We want you to know what changes will be going on. These changes happen to everyone. They are normal and interesting. They're only frightening if you don't know what to expect."

The presentation continued with the speakers reviewing the infor-mation that had been covered in the film. Maggie paid close attention to every word. She sat quietly and did not ask any questions, although many were whirling through her mind.

Maggie already knew most of the facts about menstruation and body changes for girls. Dad had told her about these. She hadn't known about the changes that boys went through. She wondered why Dad had left this part out. Maybe he had figured that since she was a girl, she only needed to know about what happened to girl's bodies.

Then she heard more of what the woman presenter was saying. "Your body belongs to you. It doesn't belong to anyone else. The changes going on in it can be confusing, but they are also exciting. You are in charge of your body. You get to decide what is OK or not OK to have happen to it."

Maggie thought a great deal about these words. She knew that if something was medically wrong, her parents got to decide that she should go to a doctor, and then the doctor got to decide what needed to happen. But what kinds of things was she in charge of for herself?

If she did not want Dad to touch her when she was drying off after a bath, could she say no to him? Could she say no to his visits at night? And would he even listen? He might get angry and quit loving her if she stopped him.

Maggie was confused. There was so much to sort out for herself. More and more she began to think that her family was not like other families. She worried that there was something wrong with her, something bad and dirty. Thoughts swirled through her head like a storm, uncontrollably skipping from one to the next. Maggie could hear her father's voice playing like a record in her head: "I love you. Touching is our special way of showing how much we love each other, Sugar Plum—but it's our secret."

Maggie's thoughts were suddenly interrupted. Sarah was sitting next to her and she was tugging on her sleeve. Maggie was vaguely aware of Sarah's voice. "Maggie, we're supposed to go back to class now. The talk is all over. Mr. Bellam's already heading out the door with the rest of the kids."

Maggie's attention was brought back to the school auditorium. Looking around her she saw that most of the students had left. A few were trailing behind the others, walking back to their classrooms. Maggie stood up to leave and started walking down the aisle to the exit.

"Maggie, you forgot your sweatshirt. Here." Sarah tossed Maggie's sweatshirt to her. "So what did you think of the talk?" she asked, quietly observing her friend.

"Oh, I guess it was OK," Maggie answered. She shrugged her shoulders in a careless gesture. "Not that big a deal."

"Yeah, I guess most of us know a lot of that stuff already. Some of the kids acted so silly, didn't they?"

"Uh-huh," said Maggie, nodding her head slightly. "Maybe they were just embarrassed."

"But they can be such babies about it," added Sarah. "I wish they'd just grow up."

The two girls silently walked down the hallway to class. Then Maggie asked, "What did you think about the part where the lady said that we have choices—you know, that we get to decide what happens to our bodies?"

"Well, I don't know," said Sarah. "I guess it's important for them to say that. You know, maybe not everyone has thought about that before. In my house my folks talk that way a lot. But maybe for some of the kids they needed to hear that at school."

Maggie was quiet. The girls walked into class and took their seats. Mr. Bellam was talking with the other kids about the presentation, asking if there were any questions or if anyone had any comments.

"There was a lot of good material that was covered today. For some of you, it was a review of things you already knew. For others, it may have been new information. We have a few minutes before it's time to go home. Why don't we talk about the presentation. I'd be glad to answer any questions."

Maggie's mind raced. She had many questions, but was not sure what to say. She sat quietly, her heart pounding steadily, each beat harder than the one before. Maggie did not seem to hear much of the discussion. She looked out the window onto the school lawn. Many of the trees were completely bare, hues of gray and brown against the overcast autumn sky. Others still had amber and brown leaves remaining on their branches. Maggie saw the thin branches moving slowly back and forth in the breeze. Dark-colored birds hopped about, every so often poking at the ground with their beaks, searching for food. Maggie noticed the brick red feathers lining the underside of their bodies. They must be robins, she thought, remembering walks with her grandfather and how he identified birds.

Emily's voice broke through Maggie's daydream. "Mr. Bellam, what did they mean, you know, at the presentation, when they said we should make good decisions about our bodies?"

"Good question, Emily. Anyone want to say what they think?"

"Well, I think they mean we need to take care of ourselves," said Jeremy. "Like eating right and not taking drugs."

"All right. That's one possibility. Anybody else?" Mr. Bellam waited for a moment. Then a student across the room tentatively raised her hand.

"What I think they meant is that we shouldn't let anybody touch us if we don't want them to," said Lisa. "Remember? The lady told us that we're in charge of our own bodies."

"Good point, Lisa. So now we have at least two ways to take care of ourselves—controlling what we put into our bodies and being in charge of how our bodies are treated by other people. I'm sure there are other ways to make good decisions about our bodies."

Maggie's attention again drifted off. She flashed on an image of her father, smiling at her and telling her she was his special Sugar Plum Princess. Maggie fought the urge to cry or run from the room. Maggie heard fragments of the class' conversation: "...body changes in boys and girls, adolescence...many questions and decisions to be made...respect for one another...asking questions if you don't know the answer...saying no if something is not comfortable...."

Maggie was jolted back into the classroom as students gathered their books and coats. School was over for the day and it was time to go home. Maggie slowly gathered her belongings. As she rose from her seat, the legs of her chair scraped on the linoleum floor and the noise sent a chill through her.

The few days that started with taking the permission slip home to be signed changed so many things for Maggie. Doubts and concerns nagged at her. The words from the presentation crashed up against her father's words, leaving her feeling helpless and bewildered. ❖

Chapter Six

Maggie remembered when she was in Mr. Bellam's class. Her confusion and fears seemed to have started at that time. One year later, she still had so much to figure out about herself, her family, and her father. And now there was this new presentation at school for sixth graders. Ms. Evans had said that it would cover some of the same things as the presentation from last year, but from a different perspective. This time they would learn more about making appropriate decisions. Maggie sat at the window, thinking how much everything had changed from a year ago. She heard the muffled sound of her parents' voices downstairs. Soon she heard Dad's footsteps on the stairs. She turned away from the window to see him standing in her doorway.

He held the permission slip out toward Maggie. "Mom told me you needed this back. Just remember, Sugar Plum, you can always come to me with any questions. You really are growing up into a beautiful young lady, Maggie."

Mom must have already talked to him about the presentation. Maggie was both relieved and surprised to see him standing there with the signed permission slip. She smiled back at him. Her face reddened a bit. Maggie did not want to let her father know that she had been afraid to ask his permission to go to this year's assembly. She quickly mumbled, "Thanks, Dad." Looking in the direction of the open books on her desk, she added, "I really need to get back to this. We have this assignment that's due tomorrow."

Her father glanced at the books. "Oh sure, Maggie. I wouldn't want to interfere with your studies." He smiled at her and left the room.

One week later was the assembly at school. Maggie attended with the rest of the sixth graders, listening intently to all that was said by the two speakers.

"Your body belongs to you, not to anyone else," the woman speaker began. "Today we're going to help you decide how you want your body to be treated and then teach you how to let people know when they are treating you in ways that feel uncomfortable. We talk about 'good touches' and 'bad touches.' A good touch is one that feels comfortable to you. A bad touch is one that feels uncomfortable. It's very important that you know the difference between a good touch and a bad touch for yourself. Good touches and bad touches may not be the same for all people. You are the one who gets to decide what is good or bad for you."

A man joined in now. "Sometimes we feel like a hug from someone, let's say from a grandparent. If that hug feels OK, then that's a 'good touch.' It leaves us feeling happy, safe, and comfortable. It's a way of showing love or caring. But sometimes a hug is uncomfortable. For instance, if the hug is too strong so it hurts or if it comes from someone we don't know very well or a person we are angry with, then you might be uncomfortable. Sometimes it might just be that we want to be left alone and not touched even by people who care about us. If that person touches us anyway, then that touching will feel like a bad touch."

"There are many different ways to set limits and let people know if we don't want to be touched," continued the woman. "One of the easiest ways for people to understand is if we tell them. We need to let them know if we don't want them to touch us. Now if your grandmother comes over to hug you and you don't feel like it, I'm not saying to yell and scream at her. What you can do is to politely and calmly say, 'I don't feel like a hug right now. I want to be left alone.' That is a way of taking care of yourself without being rude. Another kind of bad touch which we call *abuse* is if someone seriously hurts you. No one has the right to hit you or to hurt your body in other ways. Now, I'm not talking about a parent giving a light spanking. But if someone seriously hurts you, this is abuse."

The man added, "There are other kinds of touches called 'secret touches.' There are areas on your body which are private. These are the areas that a bathing suit would cover." He pointed to a large picture which illustrated this. "Touching private areas is OK when you're grown-up and showing love for another grown-up—like the way parents might show love toward each other. But that touching is done in private. It would not be right for someone to try to touch you in those areas now. In order to decide when to touch in private places and with whom, you need to be a grown-up. But it is not all right for a grown-up to decide for you right now because both people need to be involved in the choosing. While you are still young, a secret touch would feel uncomfortable and would be a bad touch. Once in awhile a person takes advantage of a child and touches them in a private area."

There was some laughter in the room.

The woman said, "Sometimes we laugh when we are uncomfortable. Bad touches and secret touches make us feel uncomfortable. A secret touch is when someone touches you in a private area and then tells you not to tell anyone else about it. Being touched in a private area when it is inappropriate is called *molestation*. No one ever has the right to *molest* you. Even though this may never happen to you, it's important for you to understand what it is and to know how to protect yourself from it happening."

Maggie felt cold. Her stomach and head ached. Her heart pounded harshly, the beating echoed up into her head.

"Now there are times when someone like a parent or a doctor may need to check your private area," said the man. "For example if you have a rash or something wrong with your body, they might have to take a look so that they can help you get better. This is different than a secret touch."

"If someone does not listen to you when you try to stop them from giving you bad touches or if they touch you in a way that seems to you to be a secret touch, then you need to tell someone who you trust. It is important that you tell a grown-up. This person might be a parent, an uncle or aunt, a teacher, a doctor, or a friend. You can also always call and talk to the police about this. Whoever it is that you choose, you need to tell them so that they can stop the touching from happening."

Maggie continued to listen quietly and watch as the speakers had students rehearse how to say no to bad touches. Some of her classmates asked questions which were answered by the man and woman.

After the talk, Maggie and her classmates returned to class to pick up their jackets and books. Phrases from the presentation played over and over again in her mind. The word *molestation* kept flashing in front of Maggie's as her thoughts tumbled about. Maggie tried to push the presentation out of her head, but the words kept coming back to her. She did not know how to put what she heard together with the touching that went on at home. Even if the touching that Dad did was not all right, Maggie did not know who she could tell or what she could do about it.

That afternoon, Maggie, Sarah, and Katie had dance class. They walked together from school, pulling their sweaters on to keep out the cold wind. Today they would begin learning dances for the Christmas recital. Now that Sarah and Maggie were in the advanced class, they were learning both jazz and ballet. In the lower level class they had only studied ballet. Maggie and Sarah would be doing a duet together and another dance with the entire advanced group. Their teacher, Jill Everett, had told them it was quite an honor to be asked to do a duet. Maggie and Sarah were very excited about this.

"I can't wait to find out what dance we'll be learning," Sarah said to Maggie. "My mom says we must be getting good to be asked to do a duet."

"We've worked really hard to learn enough to join the older class," said Maggie. "But are you sure we're good enough to be able to do this? You know, many of the kids in there are already twelve and thirteen years old. We're only eleven."

"Eleven and three-quarters," corrected Sarah. "Besides, Jill thinks we're ready. Otherwise she wouldn't be letting us try, would she? We'll do fine, Maggie. Everybody says we're very mature eleven-year-olds."

Listening to Sarah, Maggie started to relax. Sarah seemed so confident and self-assured. Maybe Jill would choose a rock number for them to dance to. Maggie liked those songs better than the ones for ballet. Dad always said that ballet was much more ladylike than jazz. He said that ballet was more appropriate for a young girl, but she thought the jazz steps she was learning were fun. They were playful and more easygoing. Dad hadn't pushed her about it. As long as she kept up with the ballet, he allowed her to continue with it. Sometimes it was difficult not to get too excited about jazz in front of Dad. Maggie enjoyed it so much that she wanted to talk about it and show the family. She knew that if Dad understood how much she liked it, he would forbid it. Right now he seemed to think that it was just a small part of class and that Maggie would outgrow what little interest she had in it.

As the girls turned the corner onto Westminster Street, the dance studio came into sight. It was a large two-story stucco building, with a sign in front that read "Everett's Dance Place." Sarah, Maggie, and Katie walked through the double wooden doors into the building. The dance studio always felt a little chilly when you first walked in from outside. Jill kept the temperature down because when the students exercised hard, they quickly became warm and comfortable.

The entrance hall that led to the locker room was covered with pictures—photographs of students performing in recitals, pen and ink drawings of dancers, posters from Broadway musicals and famous ballets, a photo of old toe shoes, and another of a female dancer stretching. Maggie loved these pictures. They made her feel like this was a world she wanted to be part of.

Maggie's picture was at the far end of the wall. She was in a pink leotard with sequins bordering the neckline. Her skirt was satin and taffeta, all pink to match. That picture had been taken last year at her ballet recital. Mom and Dad had been so proud of her that night. Dad had taken pictures of Maggie and Katie at home in their ballet costumes as they were getting ready to leave for the performance. Then he had also brought his camera to the show and taken picture after picture of Maggie and Katie as they danced on stage. After their dances, Mom and Dad had stood up clapping loudly and Dad had yelled "bravo, bravo" with a smile covering his face. Maggie had beamed back at him from the stage. That night, before they left the auditorium for home, Dad had given each daughter a yellow rose. Maggie had felt so grown-up and knew that she had pleased her father.

In the locker room, the girls changed into their dance clothes. Coming out into the hallway, they walked toward class. Katie joined the younger dance group. "Bye, Maggie. I'll see you later," she said.

"OK, Katie. Have a good class."

Maggie went down the hall and up the stairs to where the more advanced class met. She pushed open the door and walked into the huge room. On the wall to her right were big windows facing out toward the front of the building. The wall directly opposite the windows was lined with a floor-to-ceiling mirror and a polished wooden barre for holding onto when practicing ballet and doing warm-up exercises.

Maggie was the first one there. She loved this place with its mirrored walls and glistening hardwood floors. It was especially wonderful when she was the only one there—she could pretend to be a dancer performing for a vast audience. She would dance in front of the mirror, watching every move she made, making changes in her movements and imagining what she would look like to an audience. Sometimes she could almost hear the music that would be playing and the loud applause which would follow her dance.

Maggie walked across the room to the barre. She raised her left arm up with her hand stretching above her head and then bent her body from the waist over to the side, arching her arm over her head. She reached with her right arm and bent to the other side. Then she bent over, touching the floor in front of her toes, slowly stretching out her leg muscles. After this, Maggie raised her right leg and propped her foot on the barre. Bending from the waist, she reached forward, grasped her foot, and pulled slowly and steadily. Jill had told the students over and over again that stretching was essential for any good dancer. If your muscles were tight, you couldn't expect them to move in dance in the ways you wanted. Maggie wanted to be a good dancer, so she stretched.

Sarah walked in and stood next to Maggie at the barre to do her stretches. Soon, a few more girls walked into the room. Waving and smiling hellos to Maggie and Sarah and talking among themselves, they began their stretches too. A few minutes later the entire class of ten was there, being led by Jill through a structured warm-up routine.

Jill began working with them on dances for the Christmas recital. They practiced steps over and over again until their movements more closely approximated Jill's.

Jill turned on the music and said, "Now, class, let's put those steps together to the music." Maggie concentrated very hard trying to perfect her movements. The time went by quickly.

After class Jill said, "Maggie and Sarah, let's talk about your number for the recital. I've come up with a few choices for the recital. Before making a final decision, I wanted to get your input."

Maggie and Sarah smiled at each other, hopeful and excited. Jill continued, "Since both of you have been so cooperative in class and have worked so hard, I'd like to hear what your preferences are for your dance number. I think that you'll do the best job on a routine that you're excited about."

Maggie and Sarah listened carefully to Jill, nodding their heads as she spoke. "So, here are the choices. The first is a segment from *The Nutcracker Suite* ballet, the second is an easy-going jazz dance, and the third is a fast upbeat rock tune with quick-paced jazz steps. You girls could handle any of these. The last one might take a little more effort from both of you, though, since you haven't had quite as much experience with this type of routine. What do you think?"

Maggie and Sarah looked at each other. Grinning broadly and with eyes sparkling, they both announced they wanted to do the rock dance. They were so excited that they were bouncing up and down and talking all at once. Jill knew how much Maggie and Sarah enjoyed this type of music and dance in class and was not at all surprised they picked this piece. It would be a fun addition to the show.

"That's a good choice. I know you'll both put in the effort needed for this dance. Now it may mean some extra sessions here with me. We'll have to see if you can stay for an extra half hour or so after class for a few weeks. You'll also need to practice together between classes. Can you both handle that?"

Sarah answered first. "That shouldn't be any problem, Jill. I'm sure my folks won't care if I stay late to practice with you. Yours won't either, will they Maggie?"

Maggie thought for a moment. It was difficult to predict what reaction she would get from her parents if she wanted to change the already tight schedule at home. Not wanting to disappoint Sarah or have Jill change her mind about asking her to do the dance with Sarah, she said, "I'll have to check, but it should be OK. We'll work out something."

"Fine," said Jill. "Both of you check with your parents and we'll plan on starting next Monday after class. Your parents can call me if they have any questions. Otherwise just ask them to pick you up at 5:45 instead of 5:00. And Maggie, Katie's welcome to stay and watch if that would make the arrangements simpler."

"Thanks," said Maggie. "That would help. If she could stay, my folks wouldn't have to make two trips."

Maggie was already wondering what Dad would say about this. He would not be happy that she was doing a rock number, but hopefully he would not make a big scene about that. But staying late for class would mean that dinner would not be on the table right at 6:00 when Dad liked to eat. If Mom or Dad picked them up from class, they would not get home until 6:00, meaning dinner would be at least fifteen to thirty minutes late. Sometimes Dad would get angry over slight changes. He always said that schedules were very important—they helped a person be responsible and know what was expected of them. Maggie wanted to avoid upsetting her father but she was not willing to give up these rehearsals unless it was absolutely necessary.

Jill glanced at the wall clock. "It's five after five. I guess you girls better hustle and get your things together. Your parents will be waiting for you. Oh, I forgot to tell you. I have the costumes for this dance routine so you girls will just need tights and leotards. The rest you can borrow from me. The recital will be at the high school auditorium. I'll bring the costumes in ahead of time to make sure they fit you all right."

"Sounds good," said Sarah, as she and Maggie headed for the dressing room.

Jill called after them, "Sarah, Maggie, you're both doing good work. I know you'll do fine in the show. I'm proud of both of you!"

"Thanks," said Sarah and Maggie. They were both smiling. Jill's encouragement made Maggie feel happy. She felt important and good at something when Jill praised her dancing. Maggie decided she would talk with Dad and Mom later that night about the extra practice sessions. She would try to pick a time when they were calm and when nothing else was demanding their attention.

Maggie and Sarah got their books and clothes out of their lockers, put pants and sweatshirts on over tights and leotards and quickly changed shoes, shoving their dance shoes into backpacks. Katie was already dressed and waiting for them. Sarah's mother was sitting in her car at the curb. Maggie and Katie climbed in the back seat as Sarah slid in beside her mom. "Hi, girls," she said. "How was dance class?"

"Great," said Sarah. "Maggie and I are going to do a rock number for the show!"

"A rock number? Sounds like fun. I bet the two of you will be fantastic! And how about you, Katie? What will you be doing in the show?"

Katie excitedly answered, "My class is going to do a dance where we pretend to be flowers. It's real pretty music, slow and relaxing."

"Sounds good," said Sarah's mom. "This should be some show. I can't wait."

"Mom," said Sarah, "Jill wants to know if Maggie and I can stay late for a couple of times so that she can go over our dance with us. Till about 5:45, I guess."

"Sure," said her mother. Then she noticed Maggie's concerned expression in the rearview mirror. "I'll just talk to your mom, Maggie, and we'll set up a schedule to carpool later on those evenings. It'll work out, I'm sure."

Maggie sat quietly, hoping that Mrs. Bloom was right. Maybe if it wasn't a big deal to Sarah's mom then it wouldn't be for her parents either. A few minutes later Mrs. Bloom pulled up to Maggie and Katie's house. Katie got out of the car and was halfway across the front lawn, waving and calling out, "Thanks for the ride. G'night."

Standing by the car, Maggie quietly said, "Bye, Sarah. See you tomorrow." Then to Mrs. Bloom, "Good night. Thank you for the ride."

"Good night, Maggie," said Mrs. Bloom. "I'll talk to your mother tomorrow. We'll work out the new schedule. Don't worry."

Maggie walked slowly across the front yard and onto the lighted porch. Mom and Katie were in the front hall talking about dance class. Mom looked up. "Hi, Maggie. How'd your day go?"

Maggie put her things down on the small table by the doorway. "Fine, Mom. School was OK and dance class was real good. We worked on our routines for the show." With more energy in her voice she added, "Jill gave Sarah and me a choice for our dance, and guess what? We get to do a jazz number, to rock music!"

"That's good, honey. I can't wait to see it."

Then Maggie added more quietly, "Mom, the only thing is that Sarah and I need to stay late after class a few times so that Jill can work with us on the dance. She wants us to stay till quarter to six. But she said that Katie can stay and watch. Is that OK? Please? Sarah's mom said it's OK with her and that she would talk to you about changing around the carpool for those times."

Mom heard the concern in Maggie's voice. She moved closer and put her arm around her daughter's shoulders, giving her a hug. "It'll be fine Maggie. It's only a small difference. I'll talk to Sarah's mom and we'll take care of it."

"But, Mom, Dad likes dinner at 6:00. How can we stay late at dance and still stick to our schedule?"

Mom said, "Maggie, your father will survive dinner being a few minutes late. Besides, he's so proud of how far you've come with dance. I'm sure he's looking forward to the performance and will want to help in any way he can."

What Mom said made sense, yet Maggie knew Dad wouldn't be happy about dinner being late. And if he knew about the dance she was going to do, he wouldn't be looking forward to her performance either. But she would not sacrifice the rock number in order to keep her father happy.

Maggie's mother called, "Come on, girls. Get washed up and the two of you please set the table. Dinner is almost ready."

The girls walked upstairs to the bathroom to get cleaned up. Both of them had absentmindedly left their school and dance things down in the front hall.

As Mom returned to the kitchen to finish preparing dinner, she was still thinking about their conversation from a moment ago. There had been a brief burst of pleasure on Maggie's face as she talked about the dance she and Sarah would be working on. That enthusiasm had suddenly been clouded over with worry about not wanting to upset the family's schedule. So much seriousness and concern for an eleven-year-old girl, she thought. Maggie seemed to worry so much these days. Maybe it was something going on at school or maybe it was all the responsibility Maggie had taken on when her mother was sick. She hoped that Maggie would just enjoy herself and relax. The dance recital was so important to her too. She would deal with her husband and not let him put a damper on it. She was sure she could make it work out for Maggie.

Soon she heard her husband's car pulling up out front. Maggie's mother found herself moving just a little bit quicker around the kitchen in order to have dinner ready on time. At the same moment she called to Maggie and Katie, "Girls, Dad just drove up. Dinner will be ready in fifteen minutes."

Katie came thundering downstairs, jumping over the last two steps just as Dad walked in the door. "Daddy, hi! We had dance class today and I'm going to be a flower in the show. And I get to wear a purple leotard and petals on my head. Want to see it now? I'll show you. I make the best flower!"

Dad laughed. "Hold on a minute, Flower. Let me in the door first. We need to have dinner and then later you can show me."

"No, *now*, Daddy. It won't take long. Let me show you *now*."

Noticing Katie and Maggie's belongings piled in the corner, Dad said, "Katie, before anything else happens, I want this mess cleaned up. You know how I feel about you leaving your things laying around."

"Oh, Daddy. Not now, please. I want to show you my dance."

"Katie, you heard me."

Grudgingly Katie walked over and picked up her books and dance bag.

"What about the rest of these things, Katie?" asked Dad.

"They're Maggie's. But if I take them up will you watch my dance?"

Glancing at his watch, Dad said, "Well, all right, Katie. It's 5:45. I suppose we have a few minutes until dinnertime."

"See, I told you there was time," Katie said triumphantly. "I'll be right back down. Wait there for me." Katie ran up the stairs carrying both her and Maggie's belongings. A minute later she was back. She grabbed Dad's hand and pulled him into the living room. "Now you sit here," she said, pointing to the couch. "You be the audience."

Dad nodded in agreement and sat on the couch. Katie crouched down on the floor, curling up and hiding her head beneath her arms. She hummed a tune and gradually unfolded like a flower, starting by stretching her hands and arms and rocking gently to the music and finally standing up. A short ballet dance followed, ending with her curled up on the floor again. Dad clapped his hands at the end saying, "Bravo, bravo! The most magnificent flower I've ever seen!"

Katie was excited, a smile spreading across her face. "Did you like it, Daddy? Really, did you think I did good?"

"You were terrific, Katie. But now it's time to get ready for dinner." Dad got up from the couch and headed for the kitchen. Looking over his shoulder he called, "Come on, Katie. It's time to eat." He glanced down at his watch again. It was 5:50.

Dad walked into the kitchen. Mom was finishing dinner. She looked up and her husband gave her a quick kiss on the cheek.

"How was your day?" she asked.

"It was all right. Nothing special. We have a meeting coming up next week with a new client. I'll be involved in that so it may mean a few evenings out." Looking around the room he asked, "Where's Maggie? I figured she was in here with you."

"No, she's upstairs. Katie," she called, "go tell Maggie to come down for dinner."

Dad had already taken a step toward the doorway. "I'll get her." He walked in the direction of the stairs. "Maggie, it's dinnertime."

"OK, Dad. I'll be down in a minute."

"Don't take too long. Dinner's almost on the table. Besides, I haven't gotten a hug from my princess yet tonight."

Maggie stood at the top of the stairway, hesitating for a moment. Then she walked down. "Hi, Dad," she said, smiling but sidestepping him.

Dad reached out and took her arm, bringing her back over to him. "Is that all? Just 'hi, Dad?' Where's the kiss and hug?"

"Oh, yeah, I guess I forgot." Maggie reached up and kissed her father quickly on the cheek. Then she turned and headed for the kitchen. "I better go help Mom get everything on the table."

Maggie's father stood for a moment watching his daughter. That wasn't like Maggie to be aloof. Maybe something was on her mind. Or maybe she wasn't feeling well tonight.

At dinner Katie chattered on about the dance recital. Maggie was subdued. Dad finally turned to her and said, "So Maggie, tell me about your day. What will you be doing for the recital?"

"Sarah and I are doing a duet." She paused, glancing quickly over at Mom. "Jill says that we're both doing real well. She says we're ready for more of a challenge, so we're going to have to practice extra hard. She says we can do it."

"Sounds reasonable," Dad said, shrugging his shoulders slightly. "They say you get out of any experience what you put in to it. Dance is no different."

"That's right," Maggie answered, picking up on her father's reasoning. "So Jill wants us to put in some extra class time for a few sessions. We need to stay till 5:45 for a few evenings. But she said Katie can stay and watch, and Mrs. Bloom said she'll help with the carpool." Maggie anxiously waited to see what Dad would say.

"5:45, Maggie—that's almost dinnertime."

Mom intervened. "Jim, it's important. We'll all survive if we eat late on a few nights. The girls will come right home and they'll pitch in to get dinner on. Besides, I can have everything ready in the morning before I go in to work."

"Dad, please," said Maggie. "This is really special to me. Sarah and I have worked so hard to get into the advanced group. I want to do this, Dad. Please."

"All right," sighed Dad. "If it's that important. Now what's this dance you're doing?"

Maggie looked down at her plate. "It's just a dance. Something Sarah and I are going to do together." Maggie stood up and started to clear the table.

"I thought it was such an important dance, Maggie. How about telling me more about it? Are you going to do a segment from *Sleeping Beauty*?"

"No, not that one," answered Maggie, busying herself with the dishes.

"Well, come on. Are you going to give me any hints or do I just keep blindly guessing?" asked Dad playfully.

"It's just a dance with some jazz steps in it," said Maggie.

Silence followed for a moment. "Jazz steps?" Dad asked. "You're not going to do ballet for the recital?"

Maggie continued clearing the table, focusing intently on the pink floral pattern of the dishes she was carrying. "Well, the duet isn't ballet. Sarah and I are doing something different—not ballet this time."

"Why not, Maggie? I thought that's why you were going to the studio, to learn ballet."

"Well, I am," said Maggie. "I mean...I'm there to learn ballet and *other* things. Jazz is just more fun right now. Sarah and I really want to do this dance, Dad. It's fun and it's new for us. It's just something different for awhile." Maggie glanced up at her father and then back over to the dishes.

Maggie's mother spoke up now. "Jim, it's not that important, is it? Maggie's still studying ballet. She's just going to do a jazz dance for the recital." Then turning toward her daughter she said, "Right, Maggie?"

"Yeah, right, Mom. I'm still working on the ballet. We just want to do this for the show." Maggie again looked over in the direction of her father.

"OK, Maggie," he said. "Just keep it reasonable and appropriate. Nothing outlandish."

"Sure, Dad," answered Maggie, wondering what Dad's reaction was going to be when he saw their routine. He was so conservative when it came to Maggie's behavior and how she appeared to others. He was always saying things about a girl's reputation and needing to project a certain image.

Mom and Katie got up and finished clearing the table. Maggie started doing the dishes.

"How was the assembly today, Maggie?" asked Mom. "You didn't mention anything about it."

"Hey, Maggie," said Katie, giggling, "did everyone laugh when they started talking about the body?"

Katie could be so childish, thought Maggie. "Of course not," she answered. "At least my friends and I didn't laugh." Then addressing her mother, Maggie added, "The presentation was fine."

"Well, what did they talk about?" asked Mom.

Maggie wished her mother was not so interested in hearing about the talk at school. Maggie did not feel like discussing it, certainly not with the whole family standing around.

Maggie shrugged. "It wasn't a big deal. They just talked about changes that boys and girls go through. They talked about being aware of our bodies and how important it is to be able to ask questions."

"They're right about that, Maggie," Dad interjected. "But if you have questions, your parents are the ones to answer them for you.

Some things are private, you know."

"Oh, Jim," sighed Mom, "don't start this again. Maggie knows perfectly well what's appropriate or not appropriate. It's not like she's going to ask my parents an embarrassing question at Christmas dinner."

"Linda..."

Katie interrupted, "Are Grandma and Grandpa coming here for Christmas? Great! That'll be so much fun."

"No," said Mom. "We thought we'd go up to Pinewood this year. We haven't been up there in at least six months."

"That's even better," Katie squealed. She started pulling on Maggie's arm. "Maggie, did you hear that? We get to go up to Grandma and Grandpa's!"

Maggie smiled. "That'll be fun, Katie."

"Maybe we can go sledding," Katie continued. "Think there'll be snow, Daddy? Can we hike up the mountain and find a real good spot to go sledding?"

Maggie was grateful for her sister's distractions. She did not know what to say about the school assembly. She was afraid that if she started to talk about it she might blurt out her questions. The talk at school was about making good decisions for yourself. Maggie wasn't sure what that meant for her. Maybe she was making good decisions for herself. Dad said he loved her and that touching was one way of showing that. But Dad seemed to be making all the decisions. Maggie didn't really feel as if she had any choice. She had always thought that she needed to do what her parents wanted. She had to respect them, love them, and follow their directions. Dad wouldn't tell her to do anything wrong. He loved her.

But now a part of Maggie was starting to wonder what was happening to her. She felt very mixed up. Dad had told her that she was not to talk about their secret times with anyone. It was something special between the two of them. Maggie did not want to risk Dad becoming angry with her or even worse, not loving her anymore. She would just have to keep the secret and figure out the answers to her questions another way. ❖

Chapter Seven

The next few weeks seemed to rush by for Maggie. She and Sarah spent most of their free time in the afternoon working on their dance. Maggie made sure they practiced when Dad was at work. She refused to show him the dance routine, making up excuses about wanting to surprise him or not quite having all the steps down well enough to show to anyone. Mom and Mrs. Bloom alternated picking the girls up late from dance class. Katie and Maggie rushed out of Jill's studio at the end of each session. Maggie made sure that Sarah hurried too, explaining that she had to get right home to help with dinner because it was important to her father. Sarah had not quite understood this, but she went along with it because Maggie was her friend.

The second week in December came and it was two days before the recital. Maggie and Sarah were both excited about the show. Maggie envied Sarah's enthusiasm. She wasn't worried about what her father's reaction to the dance would be. Sarah's parents had both watched the girls practicing. They said the girls were terrific and that all of their hard work was paying off. Maggie was concerned that her father would be angry or disappointed when he saw her dance but at least he would not be able to keep her from doing it. Maggie could not remember ever being this sneaky with her father before, but the jazz dance was very important to her and she did not want to disappoint Sarah and Jill. If Dad was angry about the performance, she would just have to deal with it after the recital.

That night after dinner, Dad said, "Maggie, you and Sarah must have the dance steps down pat by now. How about giving me a preview of your part?"

"No," said Maggie, thinking quickly about how to avoid showing her father the dance. "I really want it to be special for the show. If I show you now, then it can't be special on Friday night, can it?"

"She's right, Jim," said Maggie's mom. "Let her keep this to herself. It's only two more days, anyway."

Maggie's dad laughed. "I give up. I'll just have to wait until Friday to see your dance, Sugar Plum."

The plan was to go to the show on Friday and then leave on Saturday to spend a week at Grandma and Grandpa's. They would have to leave first thing in the morning and drive most of the day, getting to Pinewood just in time for dinner. They would return home a few days after Christmas.

After school on Thursday, Maggie went to Sarah's house to rehearse their dance. Katie spent the afternoon roller-skating out front with Jenny. Sarah put on the music and the rhythmic drum beat blared over the speakers in the living room. The girls worked well together, moving gracefully to the music. They had mastered the movements with their hips and the last part of the dance which called for them to arch their backs with one arm above their heads in a very sophisticated pose. By the end of the song, they were both smiling broadly. They moved together the way Jill had taught them, and any rough spots had finally been smoothed out. Just to make sure they were set for tomorrow night's performance, they decided to run through the dance a couple more times. By the end of the second round, they both collapsed on the floor, laughing and out of breath.

"We're good at this." Sarah's face shone with excitement as she tried to talk in between gasping breaths. "We're really going to pull this one off!"

Maggie laughed. "I think you're right. We finally have all the steps down. If we can dance this well tomorrow, then we're all set." Maggie's face was flushed from the practice. Her eyes were bright with anticipation.

"We'll do fine," said Sarah. "Look at all the practice we've put in." Sarah paused. "Maggie, have you shown your folks the dance yet? My parents think it's great!"

"Nah," said Maggie, suddenly more subdued. "I figured I'd wait till tomorrow night."

"You're going to surprise them? What do you think your dad will say? I didn't think he'd ever let you do this dance. He's so strict and everything."

"He'll be OK," said Maggie. "He would have preferred to have me do ballet, but he knows we're doing a jazz number."

Maggie felt uneasy. She was afraid Dad would be very angry with her. She knew he would think their dance was much too rowdy and not becoming for a "young lady." There were some parts of the dance that he would think were too "sexy." But Maggie was tired of fitting the image of a young lady, of Dad's little Sugar Plum Princess. This time she was going to do what she wanted. Besides, she thought, the dance couldn't be very inappropriate if Sarah's parents and Jill all approved. Dad did not get to make this decision for her, but she still worried about what the consequences would be. Maggie hated it when Dad got angry. His lectures and punishments felt horrible. Even worse were the days that followed, filled with his silence and sulking. Then Maggie told herself that this was only a dance performance. It didn't have to be so important. Maybe she was worrying for no reason.

"Oh, Maggie. I almost forgot to tell you," Sarah said excitedly. "My folks said that I can have a party."

"Yeah?" asked Maggie. "That'll be neat."

"Wait till you hear the best part," Sarah added. "It's not going to be just a regular party. It's going to be the night before New Year's Eve. And besides that, they said that I can invite some of the boys from school, too."

"You're going to have a party with boys there? That's great, Sarah. It sounds like fun."

"But I need your help, Maggie. We have to figure out who to invite and what to serve."

"Great!"

"For starters, we need to invite Jeremy. Right, Maggie?" Sarah was giggling.

Maggie blushed. "Yeah, right, Sarah. We need to invite Jeremy.

Now who else?"

There was a knock at the front door. Sarah went to answer it and Maggie could hear Katie's voice. Katie walked into the living room.

"Maggie, let's go, it's getting late." Maggie glanced over at the windows and saw that it was already dusk. In a few minutes the street lights would be on.

"We have to go," Maggie said to Sarah. "Dad will kill us if dinner isn't ready on time. We'll finish our plans later, OK?" Maggie picked up her sweater and put on her tennis shoes.

"Sure, Maggie. I'll see you tomorrow. I can't wait for the party." Sarah was talking quickly. "Or the show, either," she added.

"I think we'll do fine. I hope everyone likes us," said Maggie, imagining how her father would react to the dance. It was too late to change it now, though.

"They'll love us, Maggie. We're going to be great!"

Katie pulled on Maggie's arm. "Maggie, we really have to go. You know how Dad gets if we're not home on time."

"I'm coming, Katie."

Sarah followed them to the door and waved as they walked down the sidewalk. "See you guys later. I'll wait out front for you in the morning."

The sky was a dark blue, the intense color just before dark. Street lights were coming on up and down Grove Street. Some of the houses along the street were dark, with empty driveways. Others had lights shining through the windows, announcing the presence of people and activity inside. The chill winter air hit Maggie's face as she walked toward home with Katie. She quickly put on her sweater.

"Race you down the hill," said Katie, looking expectantly at her sister.

Katie loved to race. Maggie used to keep Katie out of trouble by telling her that she would race her when she was supposed to go upstairs to brush her teeth or get dressed. Katie would not want to obey but as soon as it turned into a game, she would gleefully run through the house trying to beat Maggie. Usually Maggie would let Katie win.

She loved to see how happy Katie was when she finished first. Maggie felt grown-up and responsible when she was able to get Katie to cooperate. It seemed to please Dad that Maggie was so responsible. It also saved Katie from Dad's anger when she didn't pay attention right away.

"Maggie, let's go! Do you wanna race?" Katie's voice was impatient.

"You're on!" answered Maggie, laughing.

"Ready, set, GO!" Katie was off down the hill before she finished yelling go.

Maggie followed after her, running so that she was close to Katie but letting her be in the lead by a few steps. They reached their house, laughing and out of breath.

"I won! I won!" yelled Katie.

Maggie reached into her backpack and found the house key. She fumbled with the key for a moment. There was no porch light on and no lights shone from inside the house. The shadows made it difficult for Maggie to see the lock.

Finally Maggie opened the door. "Katie, will you help with the table and I'll get dinner into the oven? We have to hurry. I should have started the food twenty minutes ago."

"Sure, just let me take my stuff upstairs first. Then I'll be right down." Katie was already partway up the stairs.

"Wait," Maggie said as she handed her backpack to Katie. "Take this with you and put it in my room. And here, take my jacket too, will you?" Maggie had one arm out of her jacket as she spoke to Katie. She hurriedly tugged at her other sleeve. "You know how Dad gets when we leave our stuff in the front hall."

"Yeah, I know," Katie answered. Then in a low voice she imitated her father. "Girls, this just does not present a good image. It's important to be neat and organized. You never know who might drop in and you wouldn't want them to think there are animals living in this house." Katie giggled, amused with herself.

Maggie's impatience broke through. "Katie, please! We really have to hurry up."

"OK, OK. I'm going. I'll be down to help you in a minute, Maggie."

Maggie quickly went to the kitchen. She pulled out the casserole that Mom had made and stuck it into the oven. Checking the note that Mom had left on the counter, she turned the oven to 350°. Then she went to work making a salad. Katie came into the kitchen and began to set the table, chatting the whole time about her day. Maggie heard bits and pieces of what Katie was saying. She was busy thinking to herself about the dance and about the party invitation she had received from Sarah.

Then Maggie heard the front door open and Katie yell "Hi, Mom." Katie ran through the kitchen doorway toward the front hall.

"Hi, sweetie," Mom answered. Then she called, "Hi, Maggie, where are you?"

"I'm out in the kitchen, Mom."

Katie talked to Mom for a minute in the hallway and then ran upstairs to play in her room.

Mom went to the kitchen, walked over to Maggie and put her arm around her, giving her a squeeze. "How was your day, Maggie? Everything OK?"

"It was fine, Mom. School was good and Sarah and I practiced the dance this afternoon. Oh, guess what?" Maggie sounded excited. "Sarah's having a party after Christmas and she wants me to come. Can I, Mom? I really want to go."

"Well, when is this party, Maggie? Will it be after we get back from Grandma and Grandpa's?"

"I think so, Mom. The party is for the thirtieth."

"That should be fine. We'll be getting back from your grandparents' before then. What time is the party?"

"Sarah said that she'd let me know for sure, but she thinks it will be around 7:00."

"Seven...hmm. An evening party sounds pretty grown-up to me. But I guess you *are* growing up. Who else is invited?" Mom asked.

"Oh, lots of kids, Mom. But guess what? Sarah's going to invite some of the boys from school, too. We're going to bring tapes and dance and Sarah's Mom is going to make food. Sarah said I can help her figure out what kinds of food to serve. Sounds great, doesn't it?"

"It does sound great, Maggie. I'm glad you're going. I like to see you having fun." Mom gave Maggie a kiss on the cheek.

Maggie had been so moody and preoccupied lately. Mom had started to worry about her. But maybe Maggie was just tired or going through a phase. Maybe the time they were going to spend together over the holidays would help Maggie feel better. This party would be good for her, too.

Maggie heard Dad's car pull up out front. Katie came bounding down the stairs and was on the last step by the time Dad opened the door.

"Hi, Daddy! Do you know what? We're going to have a holiday party in class on Friday and today we got to decorate the room with holiday things for Christmas and Chanukah. Do you know what Chanukah is? I do. We talked about different holidays in class today and the different ways that people celebrate." Katie took a breath. "Michael and Ryan made noises in class and acted silly. They're such creeps! We practiced a skit that we're going to do for the kindergarten class."

Katie kept talking about her day, not waiting for a response from Dad. He called hello to Maggie and Mom from the hallway. Eventually he made his way to the kitchen with Katie trailing after him, still talking.

Dad kissed Mom on the cheek and came over to kiss Maggie who was standing facing him.

Just as he reached toward her, Maggie turned her head away and started to put the salad bowl on the table. "Hi, Dad," she said.

Dad gave her a kiss on the cheek and Maggie walked toward the table. She did not want Dad to kiss her on the lips. It was easier to turn her head away than to have to tell him no. Dad watched Maggie carry the food to the table. He was noticing once again how serious Maggie was. She seemed to smile less and less. She also seemed to be less talkative around him. Before walking into the kitchen, he had heard

Maggie and her mother talking together. Maggie's voice had sounded excited and alive. That wasn't how Maggie seemed now.

Turning to Mom, Dad asked, "Did I interrupt something?"

"Well," she answered, "Maggie was just telling me about her day and a party that she's been invited to."

"A party," repeated Dad. Then turning to Maggie, he asked, "Is one of your girlfriends having a birthday?"

Maggie turned back to face him after putting the salad bowl down on the table. "Sarah's having a party, Dad." Now with more excitement she said, "It's going to be so much fun. She's having it two days before New Year's and Mom said I can go, OK?"

"Well, I don't see why not, Maggie. Who are the other girls who will be going to the party?"

"Sarah gets to invite six girls from the school. This is the neat part. Her mom said she can also invite six boys. We're going to bring music and dance. It's going to be great!"

Dad's face suddenly looked flushed. Maggie recognized the familiar stern look as a warning of trouble. "Boys, Maggie?" Then turning to his wife he said, "You told Maggie that this was all right? Going to a party with boys?" His voice had a cold edge to it.

"But, Dad," Maggie said, "it's just a party at Sarah's house. Her parents will be there and I want to go. I don't want to be the only one not allowed to go."

"Jim, I don't see any harm in it. Sarah's parents are responsible. Besides, Maggie's getting older and there's no reason to not let her go." Maggie's mother looked confused by her husband's reaction.

"No, Linda. You're too permissive with the girls. Maggie is just not old enough for this sort of thing." Then turning to Maggie he said, "Honey, I think the answer has to be no. This is just not all right, not for my Sugar Plum Princess."

"Dad, please. That's not fair." Maggie's eyes filled with tears. She couldn't believe her father would not let her go to Sarah's party. It would be so embarrassing to miss it. All the girls would want to know why she couldn't go—and besides, Jeremy would be at the party.

Maggie's father stood quietly in the kitchen. Then he said, "Maggie, a parent knows what's best. Sometimes they have to make decisions that in the long run are important but that their children may not like. I'm your father and I know that you're just not ready for this sort of thing."

"I'm not ready for what sort of thing, Dad? A party?" Maggie's voice grew louder. She was surprised to find herself yelling at her father. "That's really stupid! There's nothing wrong with going to the party. I really want this." Maggie ran from the room crying. "You ruin everything. I hate you!" She raced up the stairs to her room, slamming the door behind her.

Dad started to leave the kitchen, saying, "I'll go talk to her. She just doesn't understand."

Mom stopped him. "*She* doesn't understand? I think *you* don't understand. Jim, she's right, you know. She's old enough to go to the party. I can't think of any reason why she shouldn't go."

"Linda, you let Maggie get away with far too much. We have to make sure she knows the rules. One of the rules is that she goes to parties when I say it's OK. Not when she decides."

"And where do I fit into this?" asked Maggie's mother. "I'm a parent, too. I love Maggie and want her to know the rules, also. But this is ridiculous. I think you just don't want her growing up. I think you're scared that she'll be a teenager soon and is becoming interested in boys."

Dad glared at her, startled by the opposition he was facing.

"Come on, Jim," Maggie's mother continued more calmly. "This party means a lot to Maggie and she's entitled to go. And Sarah's parents will be there supervising."

"I said no! Maggie's just going to have to get used to hearing no once in awhile. I know what's going to happen if you let her do these kinds of things. She'll get out of hand and want more and more freedom. Then you'll come to me wanting to know what to do about it. Well, I can tell you right now I know exactly what to do about it. I'm going to put a stop to it before it even gets started. I am not going to have our daughter going places with boys."

Maggie had come out of her room and listened from the top of the stairs to her parents arguing. Mom's tone was angry again. "You're going to put a stop to what, Jim? What is it that you're so afraid is going to happen?"

"I'm not afraid of anything, Linda. I just know how boys can be. Girls too, for that matter. And I won't have it. I won't have any of it!"

"Jim, it's just a party. All we're talking about is her going to a chaperoned party two doors up the street."

"Linda, just drop it. I said no!"

"And I say the answer is yes. She's my daughter, too."

Maggie could hear the forcefulness in her mother's voice. Dad must be fuming by now, his face a bright red. Now he would sulk around the house for days. He did not like being crossed by anybody, especially his family.

Her mother continued, "Besides, what's the problem? Are you jealous or something? You know, Jim, you have to start letting go sometime. Maggie is growing up and she's not going to remain your little girl forever."

There was silence, and then Maggie's father said, "I don't like this, Linda. But I'm going to say all right this one time, only because the party will be at the Bloom's house. If anything goes wrong though, I want you to remember that I didn't want Maggie going to this party. It's fine—you can have it your way."

Maggie was surprised her father gave in. She would get to go to the party—what a relief! It would have been embarrassing to tell the other kids she wouldn't be there, especially living just down the street from Sarah. The party would be wonderful. She would help Sarah decorate the house and get the refreshments ready. And then there was Jeremy. He would be at the party. And he wanted to dance with her.

Maggie learned against the railing at the top of the stairs smiling to herself. Then she heard her father moving through the hallway toward the stairs. She quickly ran into her bedroom, turned on her light switch, quietly closed the bedroom door, and sat down at her desk to finish her homework. Dad's footsteps were on the stairs now, slowly taking one step after another. She could hear his footsteps recede toward the den. She breathed more easily. She would not have to face him immediately.

Maggie turned her attention to her schoolwork. She looked at the assignment list she had copied off the blackboard today. She had to write a page describing something she enjoyed doing. That was easy. She would write about dance. Maggie started working on the assignment.

Her concentration was interrupted a few minutes later by a knock on the door. Before she could say anything the bedroom door was opening and Dad stood there in the doorway.

"Hi, Mag," he said. He took another step into the room and closed the door behind him. "I thought that we could talk for a few minutes."

"Sure, Dad," Maggie answered. "I'm sorry I yelled at you. I was just feeling bad. I really want to go to the party."

"I know that, Sugar Plum."

Maggie wished he would stop calling her that.

He continued. "Your mother and I disagree about the party, Maggie. But I guess since it will be at the Bloom's house, it will be all right for you to go." His voice was very conciliatory.

Pretending not to have already heard this decision, Maggie acted relieved and surprised. "Thank you, Dad! Thank you. It'll be fine. You'll see. It's just a party with some of the kids from school."

"Well, I'm glad that you're pleased, Maggie. Now how about a thank you kiss for your dad?"

"Oh, uh...yeah, sure, Dad."

Maggie got up from the chair and gave her father a quick kiss on the cheek as he bent down toward her. Dad put his arms around his daughter in a tight embrace. Maggie felt her body become rigid.

Still holding her, Dad said, "I love you, Sugar Plum. You are my princess."

Dad let go of Maggie. She made herself smile up at him. Maggie looked over at the desk and said, "Dad, I really do need to get back to work now. I have a lot of homework to finish."

"Fine, Maggie, but no more yelling at your old man."

"OK, Dad. I'm sorry."

"Now get going on that homework of yours." Maggie's father walked out of the room.

Maggie spent the next half hour undisturbed, working on her homework. After completing her assignment, she remembered she still had not taken a bath. She got her striped flannel nightgown out of the dresser drawer and walked across the hall to the bathroom she and Katie shared. Maggie put her nightgown down on the counter next to the sink. She heard Dad rustling papers in the den. Quickly she decided she should get Katie to bathe with her. That way she might be able to prevent Dad from coming into the bathroom to "help her."

Maggie ran downstairs calling, "Katie, c'mon. Let's go take our baths together tonight. Katie, hey, Katie."

Maggie reached the bottom of the stairs and went to the family room. Mom was straightening up. Katie was on the floor playing with Nelson.

"Katie, c'mon. Let's go take a bath."

"Not now, Maggie. Can't you see I'm busy?"

"Katie, c'mon. I want to get done so I can watch some TV before bedtime."

"Well, I don't want to go now. I'll take my bath later."

"Ah, please, Katie. You're not doing anything important anyway."

"No," said Katie. "I'll go when I'm ready. Just go yourself if you're in such a big hurry."

"Katie...." Maggie implored.

Mom looked over at the two girls. "Maggie, is there a problem? Katie told you that she doesn't want to go right now."

"Yeah, that's what I said, Maggie. I'm not ready to go right now."

"Everything always has to be the way you want it, doesn't it, Katie?" Maggie's tone was angry. "Well, have it your way. Who cares about you taking a bath with me anyway?"

"Well I know I don't care about taking a bath with you, Ms. Grump.

That's for sure!"

"Fine," said Maggie. "Then don't. See if I care." Maggie turned and stomped out of the room.

Maggie climbed the stairs. Katie could be such a pain, she thought to herself. She acted like a spoiled brat sometimes, never considering what anyone else wanted. She could just go ahead and take her own bath. Then Katie would miss TV because she would have to be in the bathtub when Maggie was watching her show. As Maggie got to the top of the stairs she realized that Dad might come into the bathroom while she was undressed and Maggie would be all alone with him. What was she going to do? She couldn't even bring Nelson into the bathroom with her. Katie had taken care of that.

Maggie decided she would just have to lock the bathroom door. Dad didn't like locked doors in the house. He always said that there might be an emergency and locked doors could be dangerous. But that seemed to be Maggie's only choice. Maggie certainly could not go back downstairs to get Katie. Even if she apologized, Katie probably wouldn't come with her.

Maggie went into the bathroom and turned on the water in the tub. She firmly pulled the door shut and turned the lock. She wasn't used to disobeying her father's instructions, but some of his rules just did not seem right to her. She wasn't a little kid any longer. Nothing was going to happen while she was taking a bath, nothing that would be an emergency from which she would need rescuing. Maggie undressed, turned off the faucet, and tested the water with her fingers. Perfect. It would be nice to just soak for awhile with no one to bother her. Maggie climbed into the warm water and stretched out. She leaned her head back against the cold rim of the tub and made small waves in the water by swishing her arms slowly back and forth. After a few minutes she heard footsteps in the hallway and then someone was jiggling the doorknob.

Her father's voice carried through the closed door. "Maggie, I thought I'd come in and talk with you for a few minutes. Is the door stuck or something?"

"Stuck? Uh...no, Dad. It's not stuck. It's just, I...I just wanted some time to myself. I guess I wasn't thinking and I must have locked it."

"Locked it? You know the rule, Maggie." Dad's voice sounded strained.

"Sorry, Dad. I must have forgotten. Everything's OK in here, though."

There was silence on the other side of the door. Then, "OK, Sugar Plum. But we don't lock doors in this family. Remember?"

"OK, Dad. Sorry."

Her father's footsteps retreated to the den. Maggie washed, dried off, and dressed in her nightgown. Even if she had broken the rule and lied to her father, at least she had gotten to bathe in private. Next time she would just have to be nice to Katie and take a bath at whatever time suited her younger sister.

Heading down to watch television, Maggie passed her sister on the stairs. "Sorry, Katie. I didn't mean to be so bossy."

"It's OK, Maggie." Katie looked a bit startled. It was unusual for Maggie to be apologizing to Katie, especially so soon after an argument. "I'm going to go take my bath now. Are you going down to watch your show?"

"Yeah. Guess I'll see you later."

In the family room Maggie turned on the program she wanted to watch. Nelson was sleeping on the carpet with his back against the couch. Maggie went over and settled down on the floor, resting her head on the side of his belly. The television program started. The warmth from the bath had worn off and Maggie was feeling a little chilly. Maggie's mother was folding laundry that was piled high on the armchair in the corner of the room.

"Mom, are the windows open in here?"

"No, Maggie. I closed them all just after dinner. Are you cold?"

"Yeah. I think I'll run upstairs and get a blanket."

Maggie left the room, hurrying so she could make it back to her show before the end of the commercial. At the top of the stairs she started toward the linen closet where the extra blankets were kept. That was when she heard voices from the bathroom. Katie must be in there taking her bath. Katie and Dad's voices carried into the hallway where Maggie was. Katie was giggling as Dad told her a story. Dad was in the bathroom with Katie. Maggie opened the linen closet and reached high up for the blanket. Then she heard Dad's voice again.

"Katie, do you want me to wash your back for you?"

"I don't think so, Daddy. I'm a pretty big girl now, you know."

Dad laughed. "Too big for Daddy to wash you? Nah, not that big."

"Yes, I am too!" Katie announced. "Daddy, don't. I can do it myself."

Katie was no longer laughing. Maggie dropped the blanket on the floor near the linen closet and walked to the bathroom. Knocking on the door, she opened it and said cheerfully, "Hi, Katie. Can I come in?"

"I thought you wanted to watch TV," said Katie.

"Oh, that. It was a dumb show anyway. Why don't you hurry up with your bath and we can play a quick game of cards before bedtime."

Katie's face lit up with a big smile. "Great, Maggie. I'm almost done in here."

Maggie turned to look at her father who was silently watching his two daughters. "Go ahead, Dad," said Maggie. "I'll make sure Katie finishes up in here." Then, turning to her sister, Maggie said, "We can take care of this, right, Katie?"

"Sure, Maggie," said Katie. "See, Daddy? I told you I'm a big kid now. I'm not a baby. You can go now."

Dad's mouth formed a rigid half smile. "Well, if you girls say so. I have some things to catch up on. I'll see you two later."

Katie finished her bath while Maggie stayed and talked with her. Maggie felt like a mother animal protecting her young. They played their card game. Mom and Dad were both downstairs. After going down to say good night, Maggie and Katie went to bed. Nelson was asleep on the floor next to Maggie's bed. Willie the bear was under the covers, lodged in the crook of Maggie's arm. Katie was across the hall, asleep in her room. Maggie remained awake in her bed, her mind full of thoughts about the dance recital, Sarah's party, Christmas at

Grandma and Grandpa's, Katie...and Dad. ❖

Chapter Eight

Maggie heard her mother's slow steps climbing the stairs alone. Mom stopped for a moment at the top of the stairs and then went into Katie's room. A minute later she walked across the hallway to Maggie's room. She quietly opened the door and walked over to her bed to make sure she was covered and settled in for the night.

"Night, Mom," Maggie said sleepily.

"Night, sweetie. I didn't mean to wake you." Mom bent down and kissed Maggie on the forehead.

"It's OK, Mom. I wasn't asleep yet anyway."

"You weren't? It's late, Maggie. You need some rest."

"I know, Mom. I've been trying to fall asleep. I'll be asleep soon."

"All right, Maggie." Then turning to leave the room, Mom said, "I'll see you in the morning. Have a good night's sleep."

"Mom?"

"Yes, Maggie?"

Maggie wanted to talk to her mother about Dad. She wanted to tell her about the touching. She wanted her to know that she didn't like it but didn't know how to make it stop.

"Mom..." Maggie stopped. She changed her mind. Instead she just said, "Would you be sure to shut my door? I want Nelson to stay in here."

"Sure, Maggie. Good night, now."

"Night, Mom."

Maggie's mother left the room, closing the door behind her. Maggie lay in bed awake. She stared up at her ceiling, seeing only shadows and the moonlight sifting in through the darkness. She clutched Willie to her, thinking about Grandpa and how good it would be to see him and Grandma again. She could help Grandma do the baking for Christmas dinner. She could go for walks with Grandpa along the country roads by their house and look for birds. Grandpa would tell her all that he knew about the birds. If there was snow, she and Katie could get the old toboggan out of the shed and go sledding down the hill behind Grandma and Grandpa's house. On Christmas Eve they might go carolling, all bundled up against the cold night.

Half an hour passed. Maggie's eyelids grew heavy. She fought sleep, pinching herself on the arm to stay awake. Then she heard the footsteps—Dad's footsteps on the stairs. One insistent step after another. A loose floorboard creaked. That meant Dad was almost to the top. Two more steps. Maggie listened carefully. Dad's steps faded down the hallway toward his room. Maggie breathed easier. Then the steps returned. They stopped for a moment in the hallway outside her room. Her door opened and Dad walked in. He shut the door behind him and walked across the room to her bed.

Forgetting that Nelson was there, he stumbled over him. "Nelson, move out of the way!" he snapped.

Maggie's father shoved Nelson a few feet away and sat down on his daughter's bed. "Hi, Sugar Plum," he said, seeing that Maggie was awake. "I just wanted to come in and say a proper good night."

"Night, Dad."

"Is that all for your poor, old Dad?"

He reached over and stroked Maggie's forehead. Maggie's heart pounded, her whole body filled with dread. "Please, Dad. I need to go to sleep."

"Ah, Maggie. Is that all the thanks I get for letting you go to Sarah's party? You know, I might change my mind about that. I could, you know."

The touching continued. Maggie's eyes filled with tears. Turning her head away from her father she said, "Dad, please, no. I don't want to do this anymore."

"Maggie, we're just showing that we love each other and you know that love is very important. I love you and I take care of you. You need to give love back sometimes."

Maggie's voice got louder. "No, Dad. No!"

Nelson got up and came over to stand next to Maggie. With his muzzle, he pushed at her and then at her father, concerned by the distressed tone of Maggie's voice.

Dad pushed Nelson out of the way. Nelson came back to the side of the bed again.

"Dad, please, just leave me alone," Maggie said through her tears.

Standing up abruptly, her father said, "Shh, Maggie. You'll wake your mother and Katie. You don't want to do that now, do you? I know what the problem is. You're just overexcited about the recital and the party. That's all." Then his voice got softer, "That's all right, Maggie. I can understand that. You go to sleep now."

Maggie's father left the room, forgetting to close the door after him. Maggie got out of bed and shut the door. She called Nelson back over to her. She lay in bed shivering, eventually falling asleep.

That night, Maggie dreamt that she was surrounded by darkness. Suddenly there were large hands grabbing her, many hands coming out of the darkness. The hands were hairy and much bigger than a normal person's hands. The hands kept coming toward her. In the dream, Maggie tried to scream for help but no sound would come. She kept opening her mouth trying to scream, but her mouth made only silent motions of panic.

She woke up early in the morning. Remembering the dream, Maggie felt frightened. She did not understand what the dream was about. All she knew was that it had been terrifying. Maggie lay in bed gathering the blankets up close around her. Nelson stirred on the floor next to the bed. Freeing one hand from inside the covers, she reached down to pet him. His fur was soft and warm, his breathing slow and relaxed. Nelson stirred slightly from his sleep and slowly opened his brown eyes to look at Maggie.

"Morning, ol' boy." Maggie scratched him behind the ears. "Nelson, I'm glad you're here. You're going to sleep in here every night from now on, right, boy?"

Nelson's tail wagged, swishing against the carpeting.

"That's right, Nelson. You're my buddy, aren't you?"

Then Maggie remembered it was Friday. Turning her thoughts to the present, she forgot about her dream. Friday. The last day of school before winter vacation—before going to Pinewood to see Grandma and Grandpa. Friday. Tonight was the dance recital. Maggie jumped out of bed excited about the day and quickly got dressed. It was cold this morning so she put on her pink sweats, matching socks, and tennis shoes. Opening her bedroom door she could hear the rest of the family moving about downstairs.

"C'mon, Nelson. I'll let you outside for awhile." Nelson followed Maggie out of the room and downstairs.

Maggie's mother was in the kitchen making breakfast. "Good morning, sleepy head. I was just going to send Katie upstairs to wake you. You just have time for breakfast and then you'll have to leave for school."

"Hi, Mom. What time is it? Did I really sleep late?"

"You sure did. It's quarter to eight. Did you have trouble falling asleep, Maggie?"

"A little, I guess. I'm OK, Mom."

"Are you sure, Maggie? You do look kind of tired."

"No, I'm fine, Mom. I had another one of those nightmares again, though. I wish they would go away."

"They will eventually, Maggie. Do you want to talk about the dream? It might help."

Maggie shook her head no. "Not now, Mom. It just makes me scared all over again." She did not want to think about those hands anymore.

"All right, Maggie." Mom changed the subject. "Hey, today's your big day. The recital's tonight."

Maggie smiled. "I know. I can't wait! I really hope you're going to be proud of me, Mom."

Mom kissed Maggie's forehead. "I already am proud of you, sweetie. And I'm sure I'll love the dance. I know how hard you and Sarah have been working on it. You'll be wonderful!"

She handed Maggie a plate of food. "Here, you better get started on breakfast or you'll be late for school. You don't want that." Then she called, "Katie, Jim, breakfast is ready."

Katie came running into the kitchen. She took her plate and sat down at the table. "Maggie, today's Friday! It's finally here. It's going to be great! A party at school and the recital, all in one single day!"

Maggie's father came to the table with his breakfast. "Hi, Sugar Plum," he said cheerfully to Maggie. "How's my girl this morning?"

Maggie remembered last night. Her stomach was hurting again. "I'm OK, Dad," she murmured, stifling a yawn.

Mom joined the family at the table. "She looks tired, don't you think, Jim?"

"Ah, she's all right, aren't you, Maggie?"

"Yeah, sure, Dad. I'm fine." Maggie looked at Mom. "Really, Mom, I've just been working hard on the dance. Besides, vacation is coming and I'll have lots of time to relax at Grandma and Grandpa's."

Looking at his daughters, Dad said, "Finish your breakfast, girls, and I'll drive you to school."

"Great," said Katie.

"Oh, sorry, Dad," said Maggie. "I promised Sarah that I'd walk with her today. We want to talk about the dance and make sure we're organized about our costumes."

"If Maggie's going to walk with Sarah, then I want to walk, too," announced Katie.

Dad laughed and threw his hands up in the air. "Whatever you girls want. Just hurry up so you're not late. I guess I'll head out to the office now since no one wants a ride." Dad walked over to give each daughter a kiss good-bye. "See you two at dinner tonight."

"Jim," Mom said, "remember we have to get the girls to the auditorium by 6:00 so we'll just have a quick sandwich or something before the show."

"OK, whatever. Anything for my two princesses, right? The show must go on!" ❖

Chapter Nine

The school day blurred with Maggie's excitement about the recital. The day seemed only to move toward that special event. Upon arriving home after school, Maggie said to her sister, "Katie, go put your school things away. We'll grab a snack and you can play for a little while. But remember, we have to take baths and have all our costume stuff ready to go. Mom wasn't sure if she'd be able to get home very early from work."

"I know, I know," said Katie. "You don't need to remind me."

"It's just that the recital is important, and I don't want us to be late."

"We won't be, Maggie. I have the flower wreath all ready for my hair. My tights, leotard, and ballet skirt are all together in my room."

"What about your ballet slippers?"

"Oh, yeah. I'm sure they're somewhere in my room."

"Katie..." Maggie said irritably.

"I'll find them, Maggie. Don't worry. I'm not going up on stage barefoot."

"Just don't wait till the last minute, Katie. Please!"

"All right! Just stop being so bossy. OK, Maggie?"

Instead of getting angry and yelling back at Katie, Maggie found herself close to crying. Katie watched her sister carefully, noticing her eyes filling up with tears. "Maggie?" Katie's voice was concerned.

"I'm all right, Katie." Maggie brushed a tear away. "I'm sorry for hassling you. I guess I'm a little nervous about the show."

"I promise I'll get all my things together, Maggie. You won't even have to remind me anymore. You'll see."

Maggie smiled at Katie's concern and sudden cooperativeness. "Thanks." Then remembering back to last night, to Dad going into the bathroom with Katie and then later coming into her own room she added, "Katie, I've got an idea. How about while we're staying at Grandma and Grandpa's we share a room. We could be roommates."

"Wow! Really, Maggie?" Katie was surprised by Maggie's suggestion, but she loved the idea. "We could tell each other stories before we go to sleep. And in the morning we can lay in bed and make all sorts of plans for the day. It'll be great, won't it, Maggie?"

"Yeah, it'll be fun, Katie. Now c'mon. We better get moving."

Mom and Dad arrived home early. Dinner was short. The girls barely noticed what they ate as their excitement about the show increased. Maggie's excitement was mixed with anxiety over Dad's reaction to her dance. As usual, Katie talked through most of the meal, telling her parents when she would be on stage and what parts of the dance to pay special attention to. She did not want them to miss anything important.

By 5:45 Maggie's family was in the car ready to drive to the high school auditorium. Katie continued to talk nonstop. She was so excited she waved her hands around as she spoke.

"Stop and take a breath for a second, Katie," said Dad.

Maggie thought how nice these times were, when the whole family was together and everybody was getting along. She hoped everyone would be as happy on the ride home from the recital as they were right now. Maybe she was making too much of what Dad's reaction to the dance would be. There was certainly nothing wrong with the dance. He was just a very overprotective father.

"Maggie," Dad said as he glanced in the rearview mirror. "I haven't even had a glimpse of your costume for tonight. You came downstairs with your sweats on."

"Oh...well...I just wanted the whole thing to be a surprise. Jill told us to get into our costumes at school. That way they won't get messed up during the ride over."

"Well, if your costume is in that bag of yours, can I see it when we park?"

"No, Dad. You have to wait. Remember the surprise?"

"Oh, yeah. The surprise. How could I forget?" Dad laughed.

Dad pulled the car into the high school parking lot. "Do you girls go straight to the auditorium or do you get into your costumes somewhere else?"

"Jill said the auditorium, Dad. There are dressing rooms in the back," Maggie said as she gathered her things together.

"OK, then. We'll park over there and the two of you can go inside," Dad said. He pulled the car into a parking space close to the doors. Both girls jumped out and headed off toward the brightly-lit auditorium. Dad opened his door. "Hey, you two. How about letting me give you a good luck kiss before the show?"

As Mom got out of the car, Katie came running back. Maggie followed her sister more slowly.

"Bye, Daddy. Bye, Mom. See you later." Katie beamed as her parents kissed her.

Mom put an arm around Maggie. "Good luck, sweetheart. You'll do fine."

"Of course she will," added Dad. "She's my Sugar Plum Princess!"

Maggie smiled as she grabbed Katie's hand and pulled her toward the back entrance of the auditorium. "C'mon, Katie. We better get going."

"Look for us up toward the front, kids. We'll be out there watching!" called Dad.

"OK, Daddy," said Katie.

Once inside, Maggie took Katie over to where the younger kids were changing and then went off to find Sarah. They got into their costumes and stood in line to have their makeup applied by one of the mothers. Jill walked through the dressing room, helping with costumes and giving last minute reminders to her students. She approached Maggie and Sarah.

"You two look terrific. Be sure to tell Mrs. Green to go heavy on the makeup for you both—lots of glitter eye shadow and dark lipstick. I want your makeup to really show up."

"OK," said Sarah.

"The costumes look great!" Jill added. "These skirts with the slits up the side are going to work just fine. And the sequins are wonderful! What did your parents think of the costumes when they saw them?"

"Mine laughed and said I sure looked grown-up," Sarah said.

Jill turned to Maggie. "How about your parents, Maggie?"

"My parents? They, uh...they haven't seen the costume or the dance. I wanted to surprise them."

"They must be really excited then, Maggie. I bet they can't wait."

"I guess so, Jill. Are these black tights all right with the skirt?"

"Everything looks fine," said Jill. "I know you'll both do well."

After getting their makeup and adding some jewelry to the costumes, Maggie and Sarah went to look at themselves in the full-length mirror on the wall. They started to giggle at their reflections.

"Boy, Maggie. We sure look different, don't we?" said Sarah.

Maggie stared at herself in the mirror. The makeup made her look much older, a little like some of the old pictures she had seen of Mom, right after she graduated from college.

Katie walked up from behind. Looking in the mirror, she stopped. "Wow, Maggie. You look so old like that. Like a real teenager. You guys look great."

Maggie turned around to look at her sister. Smiling, she said, "You look great, too, Katie. The flowers in your hair are really pretty."

"You mean it, Maggie? Do I really look good?" Katie's face lit up with the praise from her sister.

Maggie laughed. "Yes, Katie. I mean it. You look beautiful."

"Just like a princess?" asked Katie.

"Just like a princess."

"Thanks!" Then hearing her name being called by one of the mothers, Katie said, "See you later," and hurried over to find the rest of her group.

"Katie does look pretty dressed up like that," said Sarah.

"She does," agreed Maggie, "and she's so excited."

"I am too! Aren't you?" Sarah asked.

"Yeah! We don't look anything like princesses tonight, though, do we, Sarah?"

"Of course not, Maggie. We're not supposed to. Remember? We're supposed to look like grown-up ladies."

"I know. I guess I was just surprised to see how we looked with the costumes and makeup."

"The audience is going to love our dance, Maggie. It will be even better with the costumes. You'll see."

"I hope you're right, Sarah."

"They will, Maggie. My mom even said so when she saw us rehearsing."

"Yeah, I just don't know what my parents are going to think."

"Oh, come on, Maggie. They'll enjoy it." Noticing the lights blinking on and off, Sarah added, "That's the sign that the show is going to start in five minutes. We better go to the side of the stage so we'll know when it's our turn to go on."

From behind the side curtains, Maggie and Sarah could see the lights in the front of the auditorium momentarily go dark. Then the spotlight hit the stage, the curtains opened, and Jill Everett walked out to introduce the first dance.

Sarah excitedly grabbed Maggie's arm. "This is it, Maggie! Can you believe it's really tonight?"

Sarah's excitement was contagious. "All we have to do is go out on that stage and do it one more time. We've got it down!"

"That's right," said Sarah. "We can do it!"

"Sarah, I'm glad we're dancing together."

"Me too, Maggie. It would be a lot more scary if you weren't my partner."

One of the moms assigned to backstage motioned all the girls to quiet down. The show was starting.

The five- and six-year-olds came out onstage dressed in matching pink tights, leotards, and white tutus. They wore sparkling tiaras in their hair. The audience applauded even before the little girls did their dance of the "Teddy Bear Picnic." It didn't seem to matter that they were all doing different steps to the music. Sarah and Maggie giggled as they watched. At the end of the dance they applauded loudly along with everyone else. The little girls did a triumphant ballet walk off the stage.

"Well," Sarah said, turning to Maggie, "that's number one. Six more dances to go and then it's our turn."

"I know, Sarah." Then teasingly Maggie added, "Are you going to keep count the whole way through the show? You'll make me nervous."

"I have to keep count. Otherwise how will we know when it's our turn?"

"I guarantee we won't miss our turn. Not after all the practicing we've done. We go on right after the *West Side Story* dance."

"OK. I'll just count to myself."

Maggie and Sarah watched the next group of performers. Two more dances after this one and then it would be time for Katie's number. Maggie looked past the dancers on stage and noticed Katie standing in the wings with some of her friends. She looked so pretty tonight, dressed in her lavender tights and leotard, a silky skirt with a full petticoat on underneath, and flowers in her hair. Their eyes met and Katie waved excitedly to her sister. Maggie waved back, silently mouthing the words "good luck" to Katie. The music ended and again there was applause. Maggie watched the following dance.

Then Katie walked out onstage with four other girls. The slow music started and the girls crouched down on the stage, curled up with legs tucked under them and their heads down—just as Katie had demonstrated for Dad. As the music continued they stretched their arms and slowly got up. They danced around the stage doing pirouettes, grand jetés, and degajés. By the end of the dance, the girls were curled back into the positions they had started in. Maggie applauded very loudly, proud of Katie's performance.

As Katie walked off the stage past her, Maggie reached over and hugged her sister. "You did great, Katie! You danced just like a flower."

"Yeah, you did super, Katie," added Sarah.

Katie's face was one huge smile. "Thanks. I know you'll both do good on your dance, too."

"Thanks," said Maggie.

"Well, I'm supposed to stay with my group. I better go find them," said Katie.

"OK. See you later."

Two more dances followed. Then Sarah turned to Maggie. "This is it. Our dance is right after this one. Am I allowed to count now?" she asked teasingly.

"Yes, now you're allowed to count," Maggie answered. "I'm getting nervous. Are you?"

Sarah nodded. "My stomach feels funny and I feel like I can't stand still."

"I know. Me, too," Maggie agreed.

Jill approached Maggie and Sarah. "You both look wonderful! Are you all set to go on? You're up next."

Sarah spoke first. "We're all ready, Jill."

"Yeah, we're all set," Maggie added.

"OK, you two. Now just do it like you did at rehearsal. You were very good. Just remember, you walk out onstage and take your opening poses like statues. Then listen to the music and relax. You'll both do fine."

The music to *West Side Story* was ending. Sarah and Maggie looked at one another, grinning in anticipation. Sarah reached over and grabbed Maggie's hand. "Let's go! We're on now."

Sarah let go of Maggie's hand and the two girls walked to the middle of the stage. The lights in the auditorium were low. They took their poses. The curtains opened and the spotlight hit them. Then the music began. First the drum beat started; then it was joined by the electric piano and guitar. Maggie and Sarah danced to the music, just like they had practiced. They did high kicks with their legs and rhythmic movements with their arms and hips. The number ended with them each doing splits and then bending one leg back and arching their backs with one hand held high up above their heads and the other hand reaching far back and touching the floor. The music stopped and there was loud applause and whistles of approval. Maggie and Sarah

Reanne S. Singer

looked at one another, their faces shining with pride and accomplishment.

Sarah mouthed the words to Maggie, "We did it!"

Maggie happily nodded back to her friend. Then Maggie looked out into the audience. There in the second row were her parents sitting next to Sarah's mother and father. Sarah's parents were applauding enthusiastically and smiling broadly. Maggie saw her mother, cautiously smiling and clapping her hands. Then Maggie saw her father. His face was expressionless. His hands were still, in his lap. Maggie got up and walked off the stage with Sarah. Maggie had known that Dad would have preferred a more "ladylike," subdued dance. But she didn't expect him to be that upset about it, not even applauding. If the other parents had been so enthusiastic about her dance, then there couldn't be that much wrong with it.

Maggie felt like disappearing but she forced herself to remain and watch the next dances. She still had to perform in the finale with all the other students. Dad was not going to ruin this evening for her, she told herself.

The older kids did the next two dances. All of the girls backstage each put on a gold sparkle top hat with a matching gold bow tie that fit around the neck with a piece of elastic. As they got ready, Jill went out onstage and did a solo jazz dance. As soon as they had on their costumes for the last dance, the girls moved quietly from the dressing room to the wings of the stage. From there, Maggie and Sarah were able to watch Jill's dance as they quietly waited to go on.

"Wow, I'd sure like to dance like that someday," said Sarah.

"Me too," Maggie answered in a hushed tone. "Jill says if we keep practicing we'll be really good someday."

"I know, but could you imagine ever being able to move like that? Jill makes it look so easy."

"She's really something, isn't she?" said Maggie.

The applause for Jill was thunderous. All the girls quickly lined up for the finale with the littlest ones at the front of the lines and the tallest girls at the ends. The music from *Chorus Line* started and the girls rhythmically walked out together in two lines, one line entering from each side of the stage. The two lines moved through the dance mirroring each other, doing a can-can kick and then taking a low bow. The audience was on their feet, applauding wildly. Maggie could see her parents standing, applauding also. Maybe she had just misinterpreted Dad's earlier behavior. He seemed pleased now. Perhaps she had just missed seeing him applaud for her before. Jill came out onstage, turned to all of her students, and applauded them. The stage was full of smiles and laughter. The *Chorus Line* music started up one more time and all the performers walked off the stage, the older girls walking in time to the music, the younger children holding hands and running or skipping offstage.

Backstage, Maggie and Sarah found Katie and together they hurried to the dressing room to change out of their costumes. Then they walked to the front of the auditorium to find their parents. ❖

Chapter Ten

Maggie heard Mom calling, "Katie, Maggie, we're over here." Mom waved her hand over her head so that the two girls could find her. She and Maggie's father were standing with Sarah's parents.

Maggie held Katie's hand and guided her over to the corner of the auditorium. Sarah followed close behind them. As they got closer to their parents, Katie freed her hand from Maggie's and ran over to them, talking rapidly before they could clearly make out what she was saying. Dad reached out to hug Katie. Turning to the Blooms and laughing he said, "This one just never quiets down." Then he said, "You were beautiful up there, Katie. I'm so proud of you."

Maggie and Sarah joined the group. Sarah's parents hugged her. Mom put one arm around Katie and the other around Maggie. "My two dancers. You were both wonderful!"

Sarah's father let go of Sarah saying, "All you girls did such great dancing up there. We'll have to go see you on Broadway someday!"

"They were good, weren't they?" said Sarah's mother. "All that practicing really paid off. You looked so pretty up there, Katie. And Maggie and Sarah, the two of you moved together so well. You were fantastic!" Then turning to Maggie's parents she asked, "What do you think, Jim and Linda?"

"I agree!" said Maggie's mother. "You girls were wonderful. Don't you think so, Jim?"

Without much enthusiasm, Maggie's father said, "Yeah, they did fine." Then to Katie he said, "And look at this flower! You made such a pretty little flower, Katie."

After a few more minutes of talking together, the two families left the auditorium and walked toward the parking lot.

As they reached the cars, Maggie said to Sarah, "We're leaving first thing in the morning for my grandparents' house in Pinewood. I guess I won't see you till after Christmas."

"That's right," said Sarah. "Don't forget about the party. I'm counting on you to help me set up for it."

"I'll be back in plenty of time for the party, Sarah. I promise."

"I'll bet you will. You don't want to miss that dance with Jeremy, do you?"

Maggie feigned indignation. "Sarah!"

Sarah continued to tease, "Well you don't, do you?"

"No, I don't want to miss dancing with Jeremy. But I wouldn't miss the party anyway, even if Jeremy wasn't going to be there."

"OK," said Sarah. "Have a good Christmas."

"You too. See you later."

Maggie and Sarah waved to each other and Maggie climbed into the back seat of the car with Katie. Maggie shivered as she sat down on the cold upholstery. As usual, Katie chattered all the way home. Maggie talked to her mother and Katie a little bit about the different dances. Maggie's father remained quiet the entire way home.

As they pulled into the driveway at home, Mom said, "Maggie, Katie, I want both of you to head straight upstairs and hop into the tub. Then if you're hungry, come down for a snack and then I want both of you into bed."

Climbing out of the car, Katie started to complain. "Aw, Mom. Can't we stay up for awhile?"

"Not tonight, Katie," Mom answered. "We're driving to Grandma and Grandpa's first thing in the morning. You need a good night's sleep so you'll be all set for the trip. Besides, it's already late."

"OK, but I won't be able to fall asleep right away," Katie grumbled. "I'm too excited." She walked to the front porch, following Maggie. Their parents followed behind.

"You don't have to fall asleep right away," Mom said. "But I do want both of you in bed soon. That way you can settle in and fall asleep as soon as possible. How about if I make some warm milk with cinnamon and you can have that with some cookies after your bath? Sound good?"

"Mmm-hmm. I'm getting hungry," said Katie excitedly. "Can I have mine now?"

"No. You get cleaned up and changed into your nightgown first, Katie. It'll take a few minutes for the milk to heat up anyway. By the time it's ready, I'll bet you'll be washed and changed and ready for the snack."

"Excuse me, Katie," Dad gently moved Katie over to the side so that he could get past her to unlock the front door.

"C'mon, Katie. Let's go up together. I'll race you." Maggie put one leg in front of the other, ready to run up the stairs.

"OK, Maggie. Ready, set, GO!" Katie yelled, and ran through the entry hall and up the stairs to the bathroom. Maggie and Katie used Mom's Vaseline to remove the makeup and then quickly bathed and dried off. Maggie walked out of the bathroom first. She headed for her bedroom.

"Maggie, is that you?" Dad called.

"Yes, Dad," she answered.

"I'm in the den. I'd like to talk to you for a minute." His voice sounded harsh.

Maggie walked slowly to the den. She stopped in the doorway. Her father was sitting at his desk looking at her. "Maggie," he started, "I guess you must have already figured out that I wasn't very pleased with your performance tonight."

Maggie slowly nodded her head. She felt the beginning of a knot in her stomach. It grew, reaching upward into her chest.

"Now I know that you and Sarah worked very hard on that dance for the show. But it just wasn't becoming, Maggie. Not for my Sugar Plum Princess."

"But, Dad," Maggie started to argue, "all the other people loved the dance. There wasn't anything wrong with it."

"Maggie, don't argue with me." Her father's voice was louder now, more insistent. "I'm your father and I know what's appropriate or inappropriate for you. You're so good at ballet and it's a very ladylike type of dance. Why can't you just stick with that?"

Maggie did not respond. "Maggie! I asked you a question. I would like an answer. Now!"

Maggie's breaths were coming in short, quick gulps. She concentrated on taking one slow, deep breath. Then she answered her father. "I like ballet, Dad. But it's not the same. It's not as much fun as the jazz. It doesn't have the same, well...the same energy."

"Maggie, I don't want to see you dancing like that again. It's not right for you. And you know that. I think that's why you kept the dance a secret from me." Then in a calmer voice Maggie's father added, "We don't need secrets from each other, do we? Not you and me, Maggie."

Maggie felt uncomfortable. She knew Dad was expecting her to agree with him and to apologize. Maggie also knew if she did that, she would have to give up jazz and go back to dancing only ballet. She did not want to do that. She also did not want to give in to her father. He did not have the right to decide what kind of dance she would do. Maggie was becoming tired of him trying to control her whole life.

Maggie's voice was angry and loud as she answered her father. "I kept it a secret because I knew that you always want things your way. I didn't want you deciding what kind of dance I could do. I'm not a princess, Dad. And I don't want to have to dance like one!"

"That's enough, Maggie!" he snapped. His words slashed the air like knives. "I'll decide what kind of dancing is all right or not all right. I don't want any more arguments from you. You better go get ready for bed now."

Maggie stared at her father. His eyes steadily held her look, staring back at her, impenetrable and cold. His features looked like they were chiseled in stone. "Go on, now Maggie. I think we're finished with this subject."

"But, Dad..."

"Maggie, that's all I want to hear. I said we're done!" Maggie's father swiveled his chair. All that was visible now to Maggie was his back. Maggie looked at her father and then quietly left the room.

That night Maggie lay in bed, once again alert to the sounds around her. Over an hour earlier Katie had stopped running up and down the stairs to ask Mom what to take to Grandma and Grandpa's the next day. Her questions seemed to go on endlessly. Mom had finally insisted that Katie climb into bed and go to sleep, reminding her that they wanted to get an early start in the morning to go to Pinewood.

Maggie had listened to Mom tell Katie how much she loved her. "Now lay your head down, Katie. Sweet dreams. I'll see you in the morning." Mom walked slowly across the hall to Maggie's room. Her knock was soft against the closed door.

"I'm awake, Mom. C'mon in."

The door opened slowly and Mom sat down on the edge of Maggie's bed. She tousled Nelson's fur.

"Nelson keeping you company again, Maggie?"

"Yeah. He likes to sleep in here with me and I like having him around."

Mom smiled down at her daughter and stroked her forehead. "Maggie, you danced well tonight. I was proud of you. You and Sarah did just fine."

"Thanks, Mom. I'm glad somebody in this family liked it."

Mom sighed slowly. "Oh, Maggie. You know how your father is. He's just so protective of you and Katie. He'll forget about it soon enough."

Maggie could feel the anger inside coming back again. "I don't care if he gets over it or not. He's going to have to learn that I'm not his little girl anymore. He acts like I belong to him or something."

"Maggie, that's just his way of showing he loves you."

"Well I don't need him to show it. Not that way. He has something to say about everything I do. I hate it! I really do." Maggie brushed a tear away from her eye.

"Maggie, it's hard being the oldest daughter, isn't it? Things will work out, you'll see. Just don't make this a big battle."

"I won't if he doesn't. But he's not going to stop me from dancing, Mom. I won't let him."

"Maggie, I don't think it will come to that. Take it easy now and go to sleep. We have a big day ahead of us tomorrow." Mom reached over and kissed her on the cheek. "Good night, my sweet girl."

"OK, Mom...and...thanks for telling me you were proud of me."

"Good night, Maggie." She closed the bedroom door and Maggie listened as her mother's footsteps retreated down the hallway and into her own room. Maggie could hear drawers softly opening and closing and then the zipper and latches being fastened on a suitcase. Water ran in the bathroom. A few minutes later Maggie heard her mother's footsteps and then the squeak of bedsprings as her mother climbed into bed.

Nelson's breathing was soft and steady next to her. The bare branches of the tree outside her window scraped against the side of the house, blown back and forth by the night wind. The faraway bark of a dog filled the air. Then there was quiet. Dad must be downstairs watching TV, Maggie thought, or still in the den. Her eyes burned with tiredness. Rolling over onto her side, Maggie pulled the covers tight around her. Dad was so angry with her, he would probably stay up late into the night and then go straight to bed. He wouldn't want to be with her tonight, she thought. Not after the way she had talked to him. Maggie let her eyes close and drifted off to sleep.

Maggie felt Nelson nudging his muzzle against the covers. She opened her eyes. The room was dark. It was still night. Her eyes slowly focused next to her, to the edge of her bed. She sucked in her breath. There was her father, one hand outstretched toward her. He pushed Nelson out of the way.

"Go lay down, Nelson. Stop being a nuisance." Then turning to look at his daughter he said, "This business with Nelson sleeping with you at night is ridiculous, Maggie. We're going to have to have a talk about this."

"But I like him in here, Dad. Please don't make him leave."

Softening somewhat, Maggie's father answered, "We'll see, Maggie. I don't know." Then he changed to a matter-of-fact tone. "I thought we ought to make up, Maggie. We don't want to go to sleep angry do we?"

"Dad, I'm tired. And, we, uh...we have to be up early to go to Grandma and Grandpa's."

"I know, Maggie. But you can sleep in the car. You'll be fine. And we have all that time to rest up while we're there."

"But, Dad..."

Then she heard her father saying, "Maggie, life is give and take. You want certain things from me and I want some things from you. Like dance. You want your dance classes and for me to not tell you what kind of dance is OK or not OK. And I want, well...I just want some love from my daughter. Sounds like a reasonable trade, doesn't it?"

Maggie turned her head away from him. Cold sweat broke out on her hands. Maggie stopped protesting. She closed her eyes tight. A few minutes later, her father was out the door. Maggie was crying. Her body was trembling. She pulled the covers back up around her.

"Nelson, come over here, boy."

Nelson dutifully got up from the far corner of the room and laid back down next to Maggie's bed. Maggie stuck one arm out of the covers and reached down to pet Nelson's head.

"You're my pal, aren't you, Nelson?" Her crying continued until she fell asleep, too tired to remain awake any longer. ❖

Chapter Eleven

After six hours in the car, Maggie and her family had almost reached Pinewood. Dad drove. Mom sat in the front seat and Katie and Maggie were in the back amidst books, papers, and crayons. They took the turnoff to head up into the Sierras. The narrow, curving road snaked around the edge of the mountains, encircling their deep brown slopes. A third of the way up, patches of icy snow lay sheltered in shady spots under low-lying brush and scattered pine trees. Farther up the mountains, the snow covered more of the ground until at the top, there was nothing but whiteness, broken only by pine trees jutting out toward the sky. The day was clear, the sky a crystal blue, intermittently broken by fluffy, wind-blown clouds. Grandma and Grandpa lived in a snow-covered valley on the back slope of the mountain range.

"How much longer, Mom?" Katie asked in a tired voice.

"Another hour, Katie. Why don't you try to nap?"

"I don't want to go to sleep. I might miss seeing a deer." Then turning to her sister she said, "Maggie, remember that game where we make up stories about what we see in the clouds? How about if we play that?"

Maggie looked over at Katie. She might as well play the game with her, otherwise Katie would probably whine and complain out of boredom the rest of the way through the mountains.

"Sure, Katie. I'll play. You go first. I need some time to figure out what the clouds look like to me today."

"Great!" said Katie.

Mom looked over her shoulder at Maggie and silently mouthed "thank you" to her eldest daughter.

"OK," Katie said. "See that big cloud right in front of us? The one with the gray on the bottom and the huge white on top?"

Maggie nodded as Katie continued. "Well, it's a gigantic dog with lots of fur. Its nose is pointing up in the air like it smells something. It has a collar on and its tail is wagging. It's getting ready to chase after something. That's all. How's that?"

"Good, Katie."

"OK, now it's your turn." Katie touched her sister on the arm. Her eyes sparkled with the new game and her big sister's attention.

"Well, let's see. How about that cloud off to the left over there? That one is, umm...that one is an elephant with its trunk tossed back over its shoulder, like when they spray dirt on themselves. And the smaller cloud next to it is the baby elephant. They're both walking slowly to the river to join the rest of the herd."

Katie smiled. "Is it my turn now? Are you done, Maggie?"

Maggie laughed. "Yes, it's your turn again, Katie."

The game continued for half an hour. After that, Maggie and Katie took turns pointing out hillsides covered in snow and talking about which ones would be good for sledding. They were still talking and spotting squirrels and chipmunks scampering near the highway when the car turned off onto the side road that led to Grandma and Grandpa's.

Katie bounced up and down excitedly. "Look, Maggie. We're almost there. Mom, Dad, we're almost at Grandma and Grandpa's, aren't we? How much longer? Not much I bet, right?"

"We're almost there," Mom answered. "Another ten minutes. Can you hang on that long, Katie?"

"Sure I can. I get to carry in the Christmas presents, OK?

"Relax, Katie. Settle down." Dad looked up from the road to glance in the rearview mirror.

"But, Daddy, we haven't been here for such a long time. And look— there's snow and we can take the sleds and toboggan out. I can't wait. Maybe we can even do that today!"

"I said settle down. There will be plenty of time for all that." Dad's tone was serious. He had not talked very much on the ride from Bayview. He was the one person in the family who wasn't very enthused about the trip to Maggie's grandparents. Maggie wasn't surprised, though. Dad never enjoyed spending much time with Mom's parents. He was much quieter when they were around, keeping to himself as much as possible. When he did talk with them, he seemed too cheerful. He was constantly smiling and talking about work and all of his successes. Maggie didn't understand why her father just couldn't relax and be a part of the family when Grandma and Grandpa were around. He was always trying to impress them.

Maggie's other grandparents had died when Maggie was much younger. Even before that, Maggie had not seen those grandparents very often. They lived far away. Once Mom had said that Maggie's father did not get along with his father. She did not know the full story but she told Maggie this was why they seldom visited them.

"Look, there's the house! I see it, I see it!" Katie's voice was loud and filled with excitement. "Daddy, honk the horn. They need to know we're here! Please, Daddy, the horn."

"Katie, your grandparents will know we're here soon enough. Quiet down now." Dad's voice was irritated, with a cutting edge to it.

"Daddy, please. I want them to know that we're here."

"Katie!" Dad reprimanded.

"Mom," Katie whined as she looked over at her mother to change the decision.

Katie's mother saw her husband's sullen expression and sighed. "Katie, we'll be there in a minute. Grandma and Grandpa will know we're here."

"But..."

"Katie, that's enough now. No arguments," Dad said curtly.

Maggie gathered the books that were strewn across the back seat. "Here, Katie. Why don't you put these away in your backpack?" Then she reached down to rub Nelson behind the ears. He was laying across the floor between the front and back seats. Maggie had her feet propped up on him.

"Nelson, c'mon, it's time to wake up, guy," said Maggie as she patted him on the side. Nelson lethargically tried to roll his body, getting stuck in the cramped space where he was laying. He groggily raised his head, slowly opening his eyes.

Dad pulled the car into the gravel drive that led up to the old two-story wood house. Before the car came to a stop, Katie unbuckled her seat belt and bounced up and down on the seat. Maggie reached for her shoes. One was stuck underneath Nelson. She yanked it out and quickly put her shoes on. The moment Dad stopped the car, Katie threw open her door and went running up the three steps to the front porch. The white glider swing sat motionless, blending in with the faded white exterior of the house. Maggie and Katie had spent many hours sitting on the swing, creaking back and forth, watching birds scamper on the ground and then perch in the pine trees surrounding her grandparents' house.

"Grandma, Grandpa, we're here!" Katie yelled.

Following after Katie, Maggie and Nelson quickly got out of the car. Mom was close behind them. Dad got out and slowly walked toward the house. By the time Maggie reached the steps, the front door flew open. There were Grandma and Grandpa, smiling and arms outstretched.

"We didn't hear you drive up," Grandpa said as he gave Katie a tight squeeze. "You took us by surprise."

"That's because..." Katie began.

"Katie!" Mom warned.

Grandma quickly glanced over at Katie's mother. Then she said, "It doesn't matter. All of you are here and I love it!" Grandma reached out her arms as Maggie ran up the steps. She hugged Maggie to her. Then Katie came over for her hug with Grandpa joining them.

Grandpa laughed, and the wrinkles deepened around his mouth and eyes. "I have my two granddaughters here and that makes everything perfect." He bent down and kissed each girl on the top of the head. Maggie's mother came over and kissed both her parents. Grandma and Grandpa let go of Maggie and Katie long enough to hug their daughter.

Maggie's father walked up the steps. He kissed Grandma on the cheek and reached out to shake hands with Grandpa. Grandpa shook Dad's hand with both of his own. "Thanks for coming, Jim. I'm glad all of you are here."

"I don't know what we're all thinking of," said Grandma. "It's freezing out here. Let's unload the car and get all of you into the warm house."

"Grandpa," Katie asked expectantly, "there's enough snow for sledding, isn't there?" Katie's eyes were wide as she waited for Grandpa's reply. She crossed her fingers, hoping that this would help her wish come true.

"'Course there's enough snow, Katie. Maybe after we unload the car and warm up we can scout out a fine hill for sledding. Either that or we'll do it first thing tomorrow."

"Oh, Grandpa, I like being here so much! I love you!" Katie threw her arms around her grandfather and squeezed him tight.

"I love you too, Katie girl. Now we better help bring your things into the house before you catch cold and have to spend your vacation indoors."

Grandpa walked down the porch steps with Katie. The rest of the family went to the car and came back with their arms loaded with suitcases and jackets. Maggie was walking back to the house when Grandpa stopped her for a moment. "How's my girl, Magpie?" Maggie smiled at the nickname Grandpa called her.

"All right, Grandpa."

"You interested in any bird-watching this trip?"

Maggie's eyes lit up. "I'd really like that."

"Good. I thought so. Maybe you and I can get some special time together doing that." He bent down and gave Maggie a kiss on the forehead. Cocking his head to the side in the direction of the house he added, "I'd better let you get those things inside now, darlin'. We'll figure out a time to visit those birds later."

"OK, Grandpa," said Maggie. She started up the steps to the house.

After the car was unloaded, Grandma made hot chocolate and everyone went into the living room to sit around the fire that Grandpa had built. Nelson fell asleep directly in front of the hearth. A braided rug in pale pinks and blues lay in the middle of the room on top of the polished hardwood floor. Grandma and Grandpa had a couch and an armchair covered in deep blue fabric with small white flecks. The flecks always reminded Maggie of stars shining in the sky. Bookshelves lined the walls next to the brick fireplace. On the bottom shelf were photo albums full of pictures of Maggie and Katie growing up, along with pictures of Maggie's mother and Aunt Joanne. On a table in the corner of the room was an assortment of framed photographs of family and friends. Maggie loved this house. It had been kept the same way for as long as she could remember. She felt comfortable and safe here.

"So it's all arranged then," Grandma was saying to Maggie's mother. "You and Jim can take your old room. The girls can either sleep in Joanne's room or one of them can take the guest room if they want their privacy." Then turning to Maggie and Katie she asked, "What's it going to be, you two? It's up to you."

Before Katie could answer, Maggie quickly said, "We'll take Aunt Joanne's room, right Katie? Nelson can stay in there with us, too. OK, Grandma?"

"It's fine with me. Whatever you and Katie want."

Katie smiled at her big sister. Mom and Grandma started catching up on all that had recently happened. Dad sat quietly in a large brown corduroy armchair near the fireplace.

"So, Maggie and Katie, how did your dance recital go?" Grandpa asked. "I'll bet the two of you were wonderful."

"It was so much fun, Grandpa. You should have seen me as a ballerina," said Katie. Then she looked over at her sister with concern, suddenly remembering her father's reaction to Maggie's dance.

"I'm sorry I missed it, Katie. Maybe you'll give me a private performance and show me your dance while you're here."

"Sure, Grandpa. But I'll have to hum the music for you."

Grandpa nodded his head and then said to Maggie, "Were you a hit, too, darlin'?"

Maggie quickly looked at her father. Katie answered the question for her. "She did really well, Grandpa. Maggie and Sarah worked so hard on their dance."

"Good for you, Maggie. I'd like to see your dance, too. Think you'd be willing to show it to me?"

Maggie hesitated. "I don't know, Grandpa. It might be hard to do it without Sarah here. It's a duet."

"Well, whatever you decide, Magpie. But I'm sorry I missed the recital. If you decide you want to show me, I'd like to see it."

Maggie smiled slightly at her grandfather. "OK, Grandpa. I'll think about it."

Grandpa turned to Dad. "These are two mighty special kids you got here. You must be awfully proud of them."

"You're right," Maggie's father said. "They're turning into two beautiful young ladies."

Katie drained the last few drops of her hot chocolate. "Grandpa, can we go out now and check the hills for snow? Everything's in from the car and we've had a chance to warm up."

Grandpa looked at Katie's expectant face. "Well, it'll be dark in an hour. You won't have time to go sledding today."

"I know, Grandpa. I just want to find a good place for tomorrow. Please. That way we won't have to waste time finding a slope tomorrow. We can just go straight there."

"Katie," said her father, "take it easy. Don't bother your grandfather."

"No bother at all," said Grandpa. "Jim, do you mind if the girls and I take a short walk?"

"Well, no, I guess not." Dad shrugged his shoulders. "I mean if you don't care, it's all right with me."

"No problem for me," said Grandpa, smiling. "Katie, go get a warm jacket and some boots. Maggie, are you going to join us?"

"Sure," she answered.

"Good," said Grandpa. "Then I'm off with my two girls. I guess the rest of you will just have to find something to do without us for awhile."

"I think we'll manage, Charles," said Grandma. "Have a good time but don't let those girls get chilled. And remember, Charles, dinner will be in a couple hours. You better plan on being in by five at the latest. I don't want you and the girls traipsing around these hills in the dark."

"We'll be home before dark," said Grandpa. He walked over to his wife and gave her a kiss on the cheek. "We have to find the perfect hill for sledding tomorrow, you know. This is important work we have to do here." Stopping at the bottom of the stairs he called, "Maggie, Katie, are you ready? Let's move out!"

"We're coming," said Maggie. "Katie, here's your jacket. Are you all set?"

Maggie and Katie went outside, their boots clunking against the steps. Katie's smile was broad and exuberant as she began the outing with her grandfather. Maggie's expression was more serious. She seemed preoccupied. Grandpa noticed the difference between the two girls, but he did not say anything about it. Maybe Maggie was just worn out from the trip. If she continued looking so distant he would try to have a private talk with her.

The icy air hit them full force as Katie, Maggie, and their grandfather walked out the front door. The sky was deep blue, muted by the gathering clouds. The sun hung low over the hills, preparing for its evening descent. The clouds that earlier had been white and billowy were grayer and darker now. "Looks like we might get some snow tonight," Grandpa said. "Katie, you just might end up having all these hills being great for sledding."

"Snow tonight?" Katie's eyes were wide and glistening. "You really think so, Grandpa? If it snows, I want to watch. Don't you want to, Maggie? That'd be great if it snows! When do you think it will start, Grandpa?"

Grandpa chuckled. "Hold on, Katie. Now don't go getting your hopes sky high on it. All I said is that it looked like we might get snow...not that it's definitely going to snow tonight."

"Oh, but you know all about the snow, Grandpa. I know it's going to snow, I just know it!" Katie ran over to a nearby tree and picked up some icy snow that was laying in a patch by the trunk. She struggled to mold it into a ball, then threw it and watched it break apart on the ground a few yards away. Katie skipped ahead of Maggie and her grandfather.

"Your sister is a bundle of excitement and energy, isn't she, Maggie?" said Grandpa.

"Yeah, I guess she is."

They walked on quietly for a short time. Grandpa gently broke the silence, "So, how's my girl doing?"

"I'm all right, Grandpa."

"Just all right, Maggie?" Grandpa asked with some concern.

"I'm OK...really."

Grandpa was quiet for a moment. Then he said, "There've been some mighty interesting birds around here this year. I can't wait to take a long walk with my fellow bird-watcher here."

Maggie's face brightened. "I'd love to, Grandpa. Maybe we'll see that white owl again like we did last year, remember? We got up real early and went out just around sunrise."

"I sure do remember," said Grandpa. "That snowy owl was something, wasn't he? That owl was big!"

"He sure was," Maggie agreed. "He was so beautiful, all white like the snow."

Katie was waving her arms and calling to Maggie and Grandpa. "Look, this hill is great! What do you think? We can bring the sleds back over here tomorrow and—whoosh!" Katie made a rapid downhill motion with her hand like a sled speeding down the slope.

"Looks like a good one, Katie." Grandpa called back. Then turning to Maggie he asked, "What do you think, Magpie?"

Maggie nodded her head and yelled, "Looks fine, Katie. You did good."

Grandpa pointed to a road which curved around the hill to the right. "What do you say we keep going, Katie girl? There are more good hills around the bend, maybe a quarter of a mile up the road."

"Great," yelled Katie. "I'll beat you both there."

"I'm sure you will," Grandpa yelled. "Just make sure you stay in sight." Katie was already trotting ahead.

She soon found three more hillsides that looked good for sledding. As the two girls and their grandfather walked back toward home, they caught sight of the house through the pine trees. The sun was lower over the mountains and turned from yellow to orange and then to a reddish hue. The brilliant colors reflected upwards into the sky turning the blue to shades of purple and lavender, and setting the clouds above into deep grays, roses, and purples. With the fading light of dusk, the needles on the pine trees lost some of their vividness, turning darker, to more muted shades of green.

As he stood for a moment on the porch steps, Grandpa gazed at the deepening colors in the sky and said, "Nothing more beautiful than a sunset out here in the woods...except maybe my two granddaughters." He hugged Maggie and Katie to him. "I'm so glad the two of you are here." He gave them each a gentle squeeze. "Guess we better head on inside now. Your grandmother will start to worry if it gets dark and she doesn't know where we are." ❖

Chapter Twelve

By 7:30 that evening Maggie and Katie had already finished dinner and helped with the dishes, bathed, and changed into flannel nightgowns. They each found places on the living room couch in front of the fireplace, snuggling down under bulky quilts. The warmth from the fire circled the room in a soothing, sleepy embrace. Katie's chattering softened and slowed down. Maggie watched the dancing fire and the occasional red embers that fell from the burning logs. Both girls were sleepy after the long day of travelling. Grandpa sat in his blue armchair a few feet from the couch. Mom and Grandma were in the dining room, finishing their coffee and catching up on news about relatives. Dad sat in the brown armchair by the fireplace, reading a newspaper.

Grandpa smiled at his two granddaughters. "You girls do look mighty cozy over there." Dad looked up from the paper. Grandpa turned to him and said, "Jim, those are two wonderful girls you have there. I'm a very lucky grandpa."

"They are terrific, aren't they, Charles?" Dad said. "Maggie and Katie, you look like it's almost time to be turning in."

"Oh, not yet, Daddy," Katie objected. "It's still early."

"Well, in a little while, Katie. You and Maggie look very tired and we've all had a long day."

"How about another half hour?" asked Katie.

"All right, Katie. Then I'll go up and help the two of you get settled in."

"Are you girls still planning to share a room tonight?" asked Grandpa.

"Yeah," Maggie answered quickly, "we're going to sleep in Aunt Joanne's room, right, Katie?"

"Right!"

"You know, each of you can have your own room to sleep in if you want," said Dad.

"No, Dad. We want to share. Right, Katie?" Maggie's words sounded like an order.

"That's right," said Katie. "That way if it starts to snow tonight and one of us notices, we can wake up the other one and watch the snow together. And Nelson gets to sleep with us, too!"

"Sounds like they have it all figured out, doesn't it, Jim?" Grandpa softly chuckled.

"I guess so, Charles," said Dad, looking at Maggie and Katie. After a minute he picked up the newspaper again. "Half an hour girls, then it's off to bed."

A few minutes before 8:00, Mom and Grandma joined the rest of the family in the living room. Grandma walked over to the couch and smiled at Katie and Maggie. "You two look comfortable there. Can I join you?" Without waiting for an answer, Grandma sat down on the couch. "Linda, there's a place to sit right over here. Come join us."

Mom smiled and said, "It does look nice but after the long car ride today I think I'll do better in this straight back chair."

"Is your back still giving you problems?" asked Grandpa.

"Sometimes, Dad." Then seeing his look of concern she added, "It's not really so bad anymore. I just have to be careful. It's a little tender after the drive. I'll be fine after a good night's sleep."

Dad looked at his watch and set the newspaper down on the floor. "I think it's time for these two girls to head upstairs. Maggie, Katie, let's go. I'll get the two of you into bed."

"Daddy," Katie whined, "please just a few more minutes. You said 8:00 and look—it's five minutes to." She pointed to the antique clock sitting on the fireplace mantel.

"Katie..." Dad began.

Maggie cut him off. "Katie, c'mon. It's no big deal. What's five minutes anyway?" Then to her father she added, "Dad, we can put ourselves to bed tonight. Why don't you stay down here and visit with everyone?" Without waiting for an answer Maggie got up from the couch. She walked around the room and gave all the adults a good night kiss. Then she clapped her hands twice and said, "Nelson, let's go, boy. Come to bed." Nelson sleepily stood up, stretched, and came to Maggie. "Katie, come on," she said. "I'll even let you choose which bed you want to sleep in."

"All right!" said Katie. She gathered up her quilt, kissed her grandparents and parents good night, and then trailed after Maggie.

Katie quickly fell asleep after Maggie promised she would immediately wake her up if she discovered it was snowing outside. Maggie took longer to fall asleep. Even with Nelson and Katie in the room, she found herself wondering if her father would make one of his night visits. Mom came into the bedroom to check on them and make sure they were covered warmly enough. Maggie was awake then. Mom came over to the bed and kissed her good night, and then tucked the covers in tight around her. A few minutes later Dad quietly opened the bedroom door. He peeked into the room and then closed the door and walked down the hall to Mom's old room. Nelson was asleep next to Maggie's bed. Maggie lay in bed with her eyes open, rubbing the fur on Nelson's head. Eventually she fell asleep.

She woke in the morning to a room full of sunlight streaming in through the curtains. Katie was still asleep, but she began to move slightly. Maggie stayed in bed relishing the warmth of the blankets around her, enjoying the way the sunlight danced across the small pink and yellow flowers on the wallpaper. Katie stirred more, stretching in her sleep. Maggie was rested and alert. She had slept all night long, uninterrupted. The grogginess she felt on so many mornings was gone. With Nelson and Katie sleeping in the same room with her at her grandparents' house, maybe Maggie was finally safe. Maybe there would not be any middle-of-the-night intrusions by her father.

Katie rolled onto her side and slowly opened her eyes. Looking around the room, she gradually remembered where she was. "Hey, is there more snow? Did you check yet?" asked Katie.

"I don't know. I just woke up."

"You don't know if it snowed during the night? I bet it did! I'm going to find out right now." Katie bounded out of bed and ran to the window. She parted the lace curtains and raised the shade.

"Maggie," she exclaimed, "I was right! It snowed!" Katie was hopping up and down and moving her hands about as she spoke. "It snowed a lot! It must have snowed for hours. Look at it! I can't wait. We're going to have a great time sledding today!"

Katie's excitement was contagious and Maggie started to get excited about the snowfall. Maggie joined her sister at the window. Katie was right. The ground was covered in whiteness. There was much more snow than there had been the preceding day. The sunlight shone down on the new snow, announcing to the world that here was something untouched, waiting to be enjoyed.

Maggie and Katie dressed quickly in warm sweats. They quietly made their way to the staircase, not yet knowing if anyone else was awake. The smell of coffee wafted its way up the stairs.

"Grandma must be awake," Maggie whispered.

Katie nodded. "And I'm hungry."

The girls went straight through the living room and dining room, into the kitchen. Grandma and Grandpa were there, busily preparing breakfast. As Maggie and Katie walked through the swinging doors that separated the dining room from the kitchen, Grandma and Grandpa looked up. "Morning, sleepy heads," Grandpa said cheerily. "Did you two sleep all right?"

"We slept great," Maggie answered as she walked over to kiss her grandfather.

"And guess what?" chimed in Katie.

"Well...hmm...let me see now. Guess what, you say?"

"Grandpa!" Katie laughed.

"Well, you want me to guess or not, Katie? If I'm going to guess you have to give me a moment. I don't want to be rushed. I'm going to make my guess a good one." Grandpa's face looked serious but his eyes twinkled mischievously.

"Grandpa, I'll tell you if you guess wrong. Now guess! Hurry!" said Katie.

"All right, all right, I'm working on it."

Grandma look over, amused. She put out her arms to Katie and Maggie. "How about a morning kiss for your grandmother while your grandfather is working on his well-thought-out guess?" Maggie and Katie gave their grandmother hugs and kisses.

"Hmm...I think I'm ready for that guess now, Katie. I'll tell you what it is. By the look on your face I bet it must have snowed last night."

"That's it, Grandpa! It snowed and it covered everything outside. Come look. It's beautiful and it'll be perfect for sledding today!"

Grandpa laughed again. Maggie noticed how often he laughed and realized that she was smiling along with him. She liked the way she felt here with her grandparents. Things were easygoing and simple. She was comfortable here.

"Before the three of you venture out into that snow, you need a good breakfast," said Grandma. "How does waffles and sausage sound?"

"Sounds really good, Grandma!" said Maggie.

"Mmm-hmm. Sounds good to me, too," said Katie.

"So, Maggie," Grandma looked over at her granddaughter, "tell me about this dance performance of yours."

Maggie and Katie looked at each other for a moment. "It was fine, Grandma. Sarah and I did a number together."

"She was really good, Grandma," Katie added. "She and Sarah did this really difficult rock 'n' roll dance. They did great! I couldn't have done that dance—not yet." Maggie gratefully smiled at Katie.

"Sounds impressive. Grandpa and I will have to make it down to Bayview for your next show. You know, Maggie, I'm proud of you. I'm very proud of both you girls. I'm sure you put in a great deal of time and effort on your dances."

"Thanks, Grandma," said Maggie. "We did work hard on them. I'd like it if you could see our next recital."

"Well, we'll try, sweetheart. In the meantime, maybe you and Katie could do your dances for Grandpa and me?"

"Well, I don't know, Grandma. It might be kind of hard to do mine without Sarah here."

Grandma was quiet. Then Maggie slowly added, "Besides, I don't think Dad would like it very much."

Grandma and Grandpa looked at each other, perplexed. "Why on earth would your father mind, Maggie?" Grandpa asked.

"I just don't think he would like me doing the dance, that's all, Grandpa."

"How about if I talk to him, Maggie?" said Grandpa. "I'll clear it with your father first."

Maggie was worried. She definitely did not want Grandpa talking to her father about the dance. That would just make Dad all the more angry with her.

"No, don't do that, Grandpa. Uh...it's just, well..." Maggie could not come up with an acceptable excuse. "He didn't like the dance, Grandpa. He thought that it wasn't becoming or appropriate."

Grandma and Grandpa were very quiet. Katie stood looking from one to the other. Maggie's eyes focused on the floor.

"OK, Maggie." Grandma's words tried to soothe her. "Don't worry about it. You know how your father gets sometimes."

Maggie did not answer. Changing the subject, Grandpa said, "We better get food into these kids. They'll need the energy to keep up with me, hiking around and sledding."

Maggie heard her parents footsteps on the stairs. She volunteered to set the table for breakfast and enlisted Katie's help. Busying herself with setting the table, Maggie said a quick good morning to Mom and Dad.

After breakfast, Grandma sent the girls upstairs to make their beds. "If you look through the trunk in your bedroom, I think you'll find some old snowsuits that will fit you. And plenty of mittens and knit caps, too. I don't want the two of you spending your time here sick in bed with colds."

"C'mon, Katie." said Maggie. "Let's go see what we can find."

"Scoot off with your sister, Katie girl. We need to go outside and check that new snow," said Grandpa.

Katie ran from the room chasing after Maggie. ❖

Chapter Thirteen

The sky was shimmering blue. The morning sun was bright and persistent. Fresh snow lay like a clean sheet spread over the hillsides. The smooth surface was occasionally broken by bird tracks or the larger trails of squirrels and deer. Grandpa had taught Maggie to identify the animals by observing the different patterns in the snow. He had tried to teach Katie, too, but she was more interested in finding pine cones or watching squirrels and chipmunks scurry up the trees and chatter noisily at each other.

Maggie felt happy and relaxed walking next to her grandfather as he pulled the sled along the snow-covered road. Katie ran ahead, playing in the new snow. She was excited to finally sled and explore the woods. Nelson tramped along steadily next to Maggie, sniffing the air. He suddenly became alert when he picked up the scent of an animal or caught the abrupt movement of a squirrel dashing up a tree.

"Mighty fine dog you got here, Maggie." Grandpa nodded his head in Nelson's direction.

"He's a good friend, Grandpa." Maggie reached over to pat Nelson. "Oh, look over there!" She pointed to a tiny bird creeping sideways on the branches of a nearby pine tree.

"Just like I keep telling you, Magpie—you've got bird-watcher eyes. What you just spotted is a red-breasted nuthatch. You can tell by the bright rust-colored patch on his breast. Can you see his black crown and then a white stripe followed by another black line running down over each eye?"

Maggie smiled up at her grandfather. "You know so much about birds. Wouldn't it be wonderful to be able to fly like them—just to be free and sail about?"

Grandpa chuckled. "The flying part sounds good and I sure like watching the birds, but I'm not so sure I'd want to be one. It looks like a lot of work searching for food and trying to survive outdoors." Grandpa looked quietly at the trees. Then he pointed off to the right and whispered, "Over there, Maggie—look."

Near the base of a pine tree was a white bird about the size of a crow.

"That one's pretty, Grandpa. What is it?"

"That's a white-tailed ptarmigan. You can often find them in these forests. The sounds it makes are low hoots and clucks."

"I would love to know as much about birds as you do, Grandpa."

"Well, all you have to do is watch carefully when you're outdoors. And start reading. There are all sorts of books that teach about birds, where they live, and what their habits are. You're already a pretty good bird-watcher, Maggie. Stick with your old grandpa. I'll teach you what I know."

"I love you, Grandpa!" Maggie exclaimed.

"I love you too, sweetheart."

Maggie and Grandpa saw Katie jumping up and down excitedly. As they got closer they heard her calling, "This one. Hey, you guys, look! This is the one! This hill is perfect."

"Looks like we're going sledding," said Grandpa.

"I guess so," said Maggie. "C'mon, Nelson. Let's go see what Katie found." Maggie and Nelson ran ahead. Katie was already picking up fresh snow in her hands and throwing it high. It landed on her head and shoulders. Nelson bounded toward Katie, barking at the flying snow.

"Look at all this great snow!" Katie yelled. "Hurry! I can't wait!"

"I'm coming," Grandpa called back. "Here's the sled, Katie."

Katie ran to meet Grandpa. She took the sled from him and dragged it over to the hill. She stopped a moment, took a breath, and then tried to run up the hill pulling the sled behind her. The snow was so soft that with every step she sunk in three-quarters of the way up her calves.

"Katie," Grandpa called, "take it easy. You're going to wear yourself out before you even get to the top of the hill. Makes no sense trying to run through new snow."

"Katie," Maggie called, "hang on and I'll help pull the sled up." Then turning to Nelson she said, "Boy, you stay here with Grandpa."

Grandpa whistled to Nelson who obediently fell in next to him. Maggie was already following Katie up the snowy hill, planting her boots in the holes where Katie had stepped.

Katie waited for Maggie to reach her. Laughing, the girls pulled the sled the rest of the way up the hill. It was not easy maneuvering to climb onto the sled without letting it slide down the hill without them. Katie was in front, holding onto the sled rope. Maggie was behind her, arms tight around Katie's waist and heels planted firmly in the snow to hold the sled in place.

"OK," Maggie said. "Ready?"

"Ready!" Katie called back.

Maggie lifted her feet, resting them on the sled. The sled took off, rapidly gaining speed. Katie screamed with delight. The brisk wind blew bits of snow loosened by the sled into their faces, making them tingle with the cold. Near the bottom of the hill the girls came to a tree right in their path. Not knowing how to steer around it, they quickly tumbled off the sled into the snow. They lay there laughing. Then they got up and brushed the snow off their clothes and hair.

"That looked like some ride," Grandpa laughed. "My turn, now. Looks like you two need some pointers on steering this thing."

Maggie and Katie retrieved the sled and trudged back up the hill with Nelson and Grandpa following them. For the next two hours Maggie and Katie sledded, built a snowman, and made snow angels. Grandpa joined them for a number of runs on the sled. Nelson spent most of the time chasing them up and down the hills. Finally, they headed back toward the house, cold and hungry. They had their fill of the snow—at least for the moment.

Katie ran ahead while Maggie walked close by Grandpa. As they caught a glimpse of Grandma and Grandpa's house, Katie called, "I'm going to run home."

Grandpa waved to Katie. "Tell your grandma we'll be there soon."

As they walked, Maggie thought about her father. He had been fairly quiet since their arrival at Grandma and Grandpa's. It was nice being here, not having him visit her room in the middle of the night, and not supervising every move she made.

Grandpa noticed Maggie was deep in thought. The smiles and playfulness from just a few minutes ago were gone.

"Maggie," Grandpa murmured, "your grandma and I are concerned about you."

Maggie looked over at her grandfather, saying nothing. He continued, "You've looked so serious much of time, like you're trying to figure out something very important. I'd like to help you with it if I can. I really would."

Maggie hesitated. Maybe Grandpa was the person she could talk to. Maybe he would have the answers to her questions. Maybe he could even stop Dad from coming into her room at night. Maggie wanted to tell him what was going on.

Maggie was just about to tell Grandpa what she had been so worried about. But then the fears set in. Would Grandpa be disappointed with her? Would he think she had done something wrong? Maggie really wanted him to love her and be proud of her. She couldn't take the chance that he might feel differently about her if she told him what was going on. So Maggie decided not to tell him the secret.

"I don't know, Grandpa. I guess I've just been tired. Maybe busy figuring out growing up sorts of things."

"Well, I've gone through growing up, Maggie. Maybe I can help."

"It's OK. I think it's stuff I just need to do by myself. I'm really glad to be here with you. I'm feeling better already."

Reluctantly, Grandpa stopped questioning Maggie. "Well, if you decide you want to talk, I'm here."

"Thanks, Grandpa." Maggie smiled a little. She kept the secret to herself and decided she would just have to find another way to deal with her problems. ❖

Chapter Fourteen

Within the first three days of their visit to Grandma and Grandpa's, Maggie and Katie had gone sledding and taken long walks in the woods. The girls continued to share the upstairs bedroom. Maggie's sleep had been interrupted only by her dreams, never by anyone coming into the room. She was feeling more rested here, more relaxed. If only this could continue, she thought—maybe that was her answer! Perhaps all she had to do was find a way to stay with Grandma and Grandpa. Then her father could not bother her anymore. She would go to school with other kids who lived nearby. And Mom and Katie could come visit on vacations.

Maggie would talk to her parents about this soon. She would have to come up with a really good reason for wanting to stay. Maybe she could just say she missed her grandparents and would like to have a chance to be with them more. It would also be an educational experience living somewhere else for awhile. Her parents would like that reason. They were always talking about how important education was. Today was Christmas Eve. After Christmas, Maggie would figure out how she could stay in Pinewood with Grandma and Grandpa.

Christmas Eve was full of elaborate preparations. Cooking filled the house with a host of aromas—pumpkin pie with cloves and nutmeg, freshly-baked bread, and tart cranberries simmering on the stove. The turkey would roast in the oven the entire next day, turning a golden brown by dinnertime.

The Christmas tree in the living room was already decorated. Maggie and Katie spent a whole afternoon stringing popcorn and cranberries to drape on the branches. Ornaments which Grandma had collected ever since Mom and Aunt Joanne were children were hung amidst the shining tinsel that glistened like icicles. The girls were both excited as they eyed the brightly-colored packages under the tree, but presents would not be opened until early Christmas morning.

That night Maggie and Katie lay in their beds a long time, talking about all the things they had done that day. They tried to guess what might be in the various packages downstairs, too. Their guesses were based on the shapes and weight of the boxes and the sounds they made when they picked them up and gently shook them back and forth. Despite all their detective work, they knew they could not count on any clues with Grandpa's gifts. He always disguised his presents, packing small gifts in big boxes or making lightweight gifts heavier by packing them with rocks.

Very early on Christmas morning, Maggie and Katie woke up, put on slippers and bathrobes, then tiptoed downstairs. The house was quiet. The rule was that no presents could be opened until everybody was awake. The two girls wrapped themselves up in blankets on the couch and kept watch over the tree. Shortly, they heard a door open and close upstairs. Then they heard footsteps on the staircase. Grandpa came into the living room.

"Merry Christmas, girls. Looks like we have two impatient ones down here." Grandpa had a big smile on his face.

"Is anyone else awake yet?" Katie asked expectantly.

"I don't think so," chuckled Grandpa.

"Oh, Grandpa," Katie implored, "can't we open at least one of our presents right now?"

Grandpa shook his head from side to side. "Sorry, Katie girl. You know the rules."

"Please! Just one! Who knows when everyone else will wake up? It could take forever!"

"Katie, you're going to have to hang on a little while longer. How about you and your sister helping me set the table for breakfast? That should keep us busy for a little while."

"But when everyone wakes up we'll have to make breakfast and eat," Katie complained. "Then we'll have to wait even longer to open our presents."

Grandpa laughed. "Tell you what, Katie. How about we make some sausage and keep it warm in the oven? We can mix up some batter for waffles, too, but we'll wait to make them until after we've opened the presents."

"Sounds like a good plan to me," said Maggie. She got off the couch and went to the kitchen. "C'mon, Katie. It's going to get boring sitting out here waiting for everyone."

Katie followed Maggie and Grandpa into the kitchen. "All right, but we definitely get to open the presents before we eat."

"You have my word on it, Katie. You have yourself a deal!" said Grandpa. Grandpa began pulling out the skillet and waffle iron from the cupboard. He gave directions to Katie and Maggie about what they needed to get from the pantry and refrigerator.

Soon the sausage was made and kept warm in the oven and the waffle batter was mixed. Everyone was finally awake and seated on the floor near the tree. They opened presents, strewing paper and ribbon across the floor, and everyone was smiling—even Dad.

Katie talked quickly as she looked at one gift and then another, in rapid succession. She could not decide whether to play with her new doll, the roller skates, or the pogo stick first. Maggie put on the necklace she got from Grandma. The 500-piece jigsaw puzzle and board game from Mom and Dad were put aside to play with later. Maggie carefully looked through the book about birds that Grandpa had given her. It was a hardback copy from the Audubon Society telling all about birds in the Western states. It was a more recent edition of the worn copy on Grandpa's bookshelf. Grandpa had picked out the perfect gift for her.

"Grandpa, the book is beautiful. I love it!" she said, hugging him.

"I'm glad, Maggie. I figured bird-watching is something special that we share."

"I'm going to use this a lot. Thanks."

"You're welcome, sweetheart." Grandpa headed for the kitchen. "I don't know about the rest of you, but I think it's time for some food." The wrapping paper was picked up and everyone's attention turned to making the waffles and putting food on the table for breakfast.

"Mmm, smells great in here," said Mom.

"Well, I had two terrific helpers with breakfast this morning." Grandpa nodded his head toward Maggie and Katie. "These two girls are a big help."

"They learned how to cook when Linda was laid up," said Dad. "Maggie takes on a lot of responsibility around the house."

"Me, too," Katie whined.

"You're a big help, too," Mom added.

"You both did a fine job this morning," said Grandpa. "And now it's time to eat."

After breakfast, Maggie settled down on the couch to read her bird book. Katie switched off between jumping on her pogo stick out on the porch and playing with her new doll. The rest of the day the family played Scrabble and Monopoly, sang Christmas carols in front of the fire, played with new toys, and had a huge Christmas dinner.

That night, Maggie and Katie fell into bed, tired and happy. All that clouded Maggie's feeling of well-being was the realization that with Christmas over, they would be returning home in two days. Maggie didn't want to leave her grandparents' home—not ever.

Maggie slept fitfully, tossing and turning. During the night, she had a frightening dream. In the dream she saw a long, dark tunnel. A grate of metal bars covered the opening, and suddenly Maggie realized that she was trapped inside. It was cold and damp. There was no way out. Maggie ran back and forth down the tunnel, trying to find an escape. Small bits of light filtered in through the bars, glistening off the solid rock walls of the tunnel.

Maggie woke with a start and lay in bed thinking about her dream. She spent the rest of the night wondering how she could stay with her grandparents. She came up with reasons she thought her parents would accept, and rehearsed her discussion with them over and over again. The next morning Maggie would start her campaign to remain in Pinewood. In the early morning hours, she finally fell back asleep.

When Maggie woke up that morning, she looked over at Katie's bed and saw that Katie had already gotten up. Bright sunlight found its way into the room, sneaking in through the small gaps between the window shade and the wooden window frame. Maggie got up and raised the shade. Listening carefully, she heard voices downstairs. She dressed and walked down to the kitchen. Everybody else was up and just sitting down to breakfast.

As Maggie walked over to the table, her father looked up, smiled, and said, "Good morning, Sugar Plum. You're just in time to join us." He patted the chair directly to his right, motioning for Maggie to sit there.

"Morning," said Maggie. She sat down next to her father and looked at the faces around the table.

"You must have been tired, Maggie. It's already 8:30," her mother said.

"I guess I was." Taking a breath, Maggie continued, "I was up thinking during the night, Mom."

"What about, Maggie?" Her mother reached for the plate piled with toast.

"Well, I was just thinking about how great it's been being here. You know, being able to spend time with Grandma and Grandpa...." Maggie looked over at her grandparents.

Katie stopped eating for a moment. "It's really fun here, isn't it, Maggie? We get to sled and walk in the mountains."

"We've enjoyed having you here, girls," said Grandma. "But you're not leaving yet. You still have one whole day left."

"I know, Grandma. It's just that I miss you and Grandpa and it's important to me to have this time with you." Then looking back over toward her mother, Maggie said, "There's so much here that I like. Being able to go hiking, seeing the wild animals, bird-watching— there's just a lot to learn here."

Dad looked up from his meal and laughed. "Maggie, this isn't the last time you'll ever get to visit, you know."

"You girls are always welcome here," Grandpa added. "Anytime, you know that."

"Well...that's what I was getting to," Maggie started. "People travel all over to learn about different places. Well, this place here...I haven't even begun to learn all that I can here." Gathering more courage she added, "Just think how much more I could learn about the seasons and wildlife if I had the chance to spend more time here."

Mom looked concerned. "Maggie, you know we have to head home tomorrow. Dad and I both have to get back to work. You and Katie have school starting right after New Year's. We'll come back soon, honey. Or maybe Grandma and Grandpa will come down for a visit with us."

"But that's what I'm trying to say, Mom. I don't want to leave. I want to stay here."

"For how long?" Katie questioned. "School starts soon. If Maggie gets to miss school then I do, too!" Once again, Katie was ignored.

"Maggie, your mother just explained this to you. We have to get back home. We can't stay on vacation forever." Dad shrugged his shoulders and shook his head. Looking at Maggie's grandparents he said, "Kids—they think life is one big party and you can just play all the time."

Maggie was getting frustrated. She felt humiliated by her father's teasing. "That's not what I mean! I know you and Mom need to get back home. But I don't." Now Maggie looked at her mother, deliberately avoiding her father. "I don't want to go home," she continued seriously. "I want to stay here."

"Do you mean you want to stay here until school starts?" asked Maggie's grandfather.

Maggie shook her head slowly from side to side. In a soft voice she said, "No, Grandpa. That's not what I mean. I want to stay and go to school here."

Everyone at the table was quiet. Maggie's grandparents briefly looked at each other. Katie looked from face to face, confused about why Maggie was making such a big deal about this. Maggie's mother was the first one to speak. "Maggie, what about school and all your friends? We'd miss you, honey."

In an exasperated tone, Maggie's father broke in. "I don't know what this conversation is all about, Maggie. But you can stop it right now. It's just out of the question, pure and simple. We leave for home tomorrow and you're going with us." He picked up his fork and started eating breakfast again.

"But, Dad," Maggie implored, "I'm not talking about forever. I just want to stay for awhile."

"Maggie, that's enough!" Dad's voice was stern. "Settle down and eat your breakfast. Now!"

Maggie pushed her chair away from the table and stood up abruptly. "I'm not hungry." Looking at her father she added, "I'm growing up and I should be able to make some decisions for myself. I can't stay your princess forever, you know!"

"Maggie," Mom said, "there's no call for rudeness here. Your father said no, and I agree with him."

Maggie's eyes filled with tears. She reached up with one hand and wiped the tears from her cheek. "You don't understand, Mom! You just don't see anything, do you? Not ever! You don't even understand about your own family!"

"Maggie!" her father reprimanded as he flashed her a glance that clearly told her to be quiet. Turning pale, Maggie realized she had almost revealed the secret. She turned and ran from the room.

An awkward silence engulfed the kitchen. Finally Grandpa said, "You know, Jim and Linda, I don't want to interfere, but maybe Maggie does need a change. For this whole visit, she's looked like something is troubling her. Maybe she could just stay with us until summer and finish out the school year here if that's what she wants."

Dad smiled offhandedly at his father-in-law. "Charles, you know how kids are. One minute they say they want one thing and the next minute it's something else. Maggie has just gotten this whim into her head and she'll get over it. We're not going to make any decisions just because she decides this is what she wants."

"Well, I'm just offering. It would certainly be fine with us," Grandpa said as he looked to Grandma for agreement. Grandma nodded her head.

"Jim," Linda interjected, "maybe we should talk some more about this idea of Maggie's. It seems so important to her. I can't remember when I've seen her this upset. Maybe it would be good for her to get away for awhile."

Katie suddenly chimed in. "If Maggie's going to stay then I get to. It's no fair if she gets to stay and play in the snow every day and I have to go home to boring Bayview."

"No one is staying here." Dad sounded very annoyed. "Katie, you're going home and so is your sister." Dad glared at Mom and added, "Linda, I can't believe that you're even considering this. Maggie is coming home with us and that's the end of it. Now, may I please eat my breakfast?"

Breakfast was finished with little further conversation. Maggie kept to herself for the rest of the morning, declining her mother's efforts to include her in activities and refusing an invitation from Katie to go sledding. In the late morning, Maggie's father came upstairs. Opening the bedroom door, he walked inside and stood looking at his daughter. "Maggie, how about coming down and joining the rest of us?"

"Not right now, Dad."

"Maggie, you can't just sit up here all day long because you're not getting your own way on this ridiculous idea of yours."

Maggie looked up and stared silently at her father.

"Maggie, I just don't understand you sometimes. This is absurd. If you want to sulk around the house all day, I guess I won't force you to do otherwise. But I want to tell you, young lady, I am not at all pleased with this behavior."

"Dad," Maggie begged, "I just want to stay here. I don't know why it has to be such a big deal. Grandma and Grandpa will say yes if you and Mom do. They would take care of me and I could go to school here."

Dad's face reddened. "Maggie, that's enough of this!" His voice was strong and angry. "I don't know what's going on with you but you're my daughter and you belong at home with your mother and me.

Now...tomorrow morning we leave for home. And you'll be in the car with us. That's the end of it, Maggie. I don't want to hear anymore about it!" He turned and walked from the room, slamming the door loudly behind him.

Maggie remained in the bedroom through lunchtime. Finally in the afternoon, she ventured out of the house for a walk with Grandpa and Nelson.

"Maggie," said Grandpa gently, "you know you and your sister can come visit here anytime, as long as your parents say that it's all right."

"I know, Grandpa. But I don't want to visit. I want to stay. I just want to be away from home for awhile."

Grandpa continued in a soft voice. "Maggie, usually when people want to be away from home there's a reason. Does this have anything to do with your Dad's reaction to that dance you were in?"

Maggie shook her head. "No, Grandpa. It's not that. It's just that I..."

Maggie stopped. Again she was faced with the question of whether or not to tell her grandfather the truth. Even if she did tell him, Dad would just say that she was lying because she wanted to stay here. Grandpa would be in the middle of a fight with Dad. Or worse, he might not believe her.

"I'm just tired of him treating me like a little girl all the time. He has an opinion about everything I do."

"Oh, yes. Fathers get like that, don't they? Believe it or not, I'll bet your mother felt the same way about me at times."

"You couldn't have been as bad as my dad is," Maggie said with conviction. "No one is as bossy as he is!"

"Well, I don't know about that, Maggie. He's probably just having a rough time realizing how fast you're growing up. It's hard being a father, you know. Come on. Cheer up, Maggie. Tell you what. How about if your grandma and I come for a visit at the beginning of the summer? Maybe you and Katie can drive back with us and spend part of the summer here."

"Grandpa, I'd like to come stay this summer. But you don't understand. It's...it's just important to be able to do it now. It was going to make things simpler for me."

"Maggie, you heard your father. I can't change his mind, even though I sure would love having you here. But your parents would miss you. You know, I can't blame them for wanting you to be at home."

Maggie wanted to blurt the truth out to her grandfather but the words would not come. They remained deep within her, feeling like a lead weight at the bottom of her stomach.

Grandpa tried to cheer her up. "Summer's not that far away. Just you wait. It'll be here in no time. We'll get you up here for a visit."

"Yeah, sure," Maggie answered sarcastically. Fighting back her tears she asked, "Who's going to convince my father about that?"

Grandpa was alarmed at Maggie's tone of voice. It was so unlike her. He tried to reassure her. "I'll help you, Maggie. I bet I can take care of that one with your father. Besides, school won't be in session then so your parents won't have to worry about you missing it. And they wouldn't have to worry about you and your sister during the summer when school's out and they're at work. OK? How about a smile and a big hug now?"

Maggie gave him a half-smile. Grandpa put his arms around her and gave her a hug. "That's a start, darlin'. But in my time I've definitely seen better smiles than that one."

"I love you, Grandpa," said Maggie. She hugged him back.

"I know, Maggie. I love you, too." ❖

Chapter Fifteen

It was late at night. The house was still. Katie lay quietly sleeping in her bed. Nelson was curled up between the two beds, moving slightly in his sleep. Maggie's parents and grandparents had gone to bed several hours ago. Maggie could not sleep, however. She sat by the bedroom window and stared into the darkness. The forest surrounding her grandparents' house looked like dark lines etched in charcoal against the hazy gray shadows of the night. Every so often Maggie heard the scratching of a raccoon's claws and the solitary call of an owl.

Maggie turned away from the window and looked around the bedroom. This room and her grandparents' house had been safe for her. Maggie knew she had to go home. Maggie felt angry as she thought about leaving Grandma and Grandpa's. Dad could force her to go home, but she was determined to find a way to stop his night visits. There had to be *some* way.

Maggie's gaze fell on Katie, asleep nearby. That was it—Katie was the answer! Katie had shared this room with Maggie during Christmas vacation. Dad had not bothered Maggie the whole time they had been here. So that must be the solution. Maggie would invite Katie to share her bedroom with her at home. She was sure that Katie would agree. In fact, Katie would be thrilled. She always seemed to want to be around Maggie and it wouldn't be so bad. Katie had been more fun to be around lately, not acting so babyish the way she used to. Besides, that would prevent Dad from bothering either one of them. Maggie crawled back in bed and tried to get warm between the cold sheets.

Morning came quickly. Maggie woke up feeling groggy. Katie was already out of bed and packing her suitcase.

"Hi," said Katie. "Breakfast is almost ready downstairs. Dad wants us packed and ready to go after breakfast."

"OK, Katie," said Maggie. She was annoyed with her father's orders. Then she remembered her plan from last night. Sitting up in bed she said, "Katie...I was thinking. You know, I've liked sharing a room with you while we've been here."

"You have?" Katie looked pleased but a little surprised.

"Mmm-hmm. And I was thinking, when we get home, instead of staying in separate rooms like we always do, what if we share a room? We could be roommates."

Katie scrunched her eyebrows together. "You mean sleep in the same bedroom? Both of us?"

Maggie laughed. "Yeah. It would be fun. We could still keep our own things in our own rooms. That way we could have our separate places for doing homework or playing, but we could have each other for company during the night."

Katie smiled, thinking about her sister's plan. "It sounds good to me. Which room would we sleep in?"

"Your choice," said Maggie.

"Then I pick your room," said Katie. "Can Nelson still sleep in there with us?"

"Sure, it's now his room, too."

"You've got yourself a deal!" Katie sounded triumphant. She came across the room and hugged Maggie. "This will be great," she said. "Thanks, Maggie."

Katie excitedly ran from the room to go tell everyone. Before she had even gotten downstairs she was yelling, "Mom, Dad, guess what? Maggie and I are going to share a bedroom at home!"

Maggie was at the top of the stairs when Dad met Katie at the foot of the stairs. "What's all the noise about, Katie?"

"Dad, guess what? Maggie and I are going to be roommates. Nelson, too! Isn't that terrific?"

Maggie could see her father standing quietly and staring at Katie. "Daddy, isn't that great?" Katie continued. "Maggie and I decided that we're going to share her bedroom when we get home. What do you think?"

"Oh...I...I think we need to talk this one over a bit first, Katie." Dad looked up and saw Maggie standing at the top of the stairs. Looking straight at her for a moment, he continued, "I think we'll definitely have to think this one through. Your mother and I will discuss it."

"But Daddy, it's a great idea. And Maggie and I both really want to." Katie begged.

Walking in from the kitchen, Mom said, "What's going on out here? Sounds like something important to me."

Katie said excitedly, "Mom, Maggie said that she and I can share a room at home and..." Katie paused, anxiously looking over at her father. "And Daddy said that he doesn't know if it's OK and that he has to talk to you about it."

Maggie came down the stairs with Nelson right behind her. "Morning, everyone," she said cheerfully. Looking directly at her mother she continued, "Katie and I really want to share a bedroom, Mom. We've already got it all figured out. We can sleep in my room at night, with Nelson of course. But we can still keep our own stuff in separate rooms so if we want to study alone or play with friends by ourselves we can do that, too. Don't you think that's a great idea?"

Mom shrugged and laughed. "Sounds fine to me if that's what you two girls want. In fact, I think it's nice that you're getting along together so well and want to be with each other more. Don't you think so, Jim?" she said as she turned to look at her husband.

"I just don't understand it, that's all, Linda. I don't know that it's the best idea. We'll have the girls laying awake and chatting till who knows when. And you know how they get without enough sleep."

"They seemed to do all right here, Jim. I don't really think it'll be a problem."

"Dad, we'll be fine," Maggie interjected. "We haven't been staying up late talking, have we, Katie?"

"Uh-uh," Katie shook her head. Then looking at her father she begged, "Please, Daddy, please. It'll work. You'll see."

"I guess I'm out voted," he said. Staring at Maggie for a long moment, he turned and left the room.

"Well, girls," said Mom, "breakfast will get cold. And besides, your father wants to get an early start home. We better get you two fed and dressed."

Mom walked back toward the kitchen. Maggie and Katie smiled at each other.

"We did it!" said Maggie, proud of her success. "We're all set!"

"Yeah," agreed Katie. "We're all set!"

After breakfast, Mom and Dad packed the car. Everyone was out on the front porch saying their good-byes. Grandma and Grandpa gave big hugs and kisses to both girls. Some of the panic Maggie felt about going home had subsided with the new plan of rooming with Katie.

Grandpa bent down and held Maggie close to him. "Remember the summer, Magpie," he whispered. "Grandma and I will be down in June. And don't worry about your father. I'll take care of things with him. I love you."

"I love you too, Grandpa."

Maggie and Katie climbed into the back seat of the station wagon. "Here, Nelson," Maggie called. "C'mon, boy."

Nelson ran toward the car, clumsily climbing in and trying to fit his large body into the small space left for him.

"Bye, Mom. Bye, Dad," said Maggie's mother as she kissed both her parents. "Happy New Year and thanks for everything. We had a wonderful time."

"We did too," said Grandma. "I'm glad you came."

Maggie's father gave Grandma a quick kiss on the cheek and shook hands with Grandpa. Grandpa said, "Take care of those two girls for me, Jim. You drive safe."

"I will," said Dad, "on both counts." Then, as an afterthought he added, "Have a good New Year."

"Happy New Year," answered Grandpa.

Dad climbed in the car. "All ready," he announced and started the car. Maggie and Katie waved to their grandparents who stood on the porch watching them drive away. Maggie continued looking at her grandparents and the house that had been a haven for her. She felt sad leaving, but she was calmer now than the day before. She kept looking out the back window until the car rounded a bend, blocking her grandparents and their house from view. ❖

Chapter Sixteen

As they headed back to Bayview, Maggie thought a lot about Sarah's party. With all the excitement of Christmas and visiting her grandparents, Maggie had not thought much about it. When Maggie got home, Sarah asked for her help in planning all the details. They had to decide what kind of food to serve, what decorations to put up, what music to play, and most importantly, what to wear. Maggie was soon caught up in Sarah's enthusiasm. She was careful, however, not to show too much excitement about the party in front of her father. She did not want to remind him too much about the party and take the chance that he would change his mind and keep her from going.

Maggie spent the day of the party with Sarah, decorating her house and preparing food. They crisscrossed bright pink and purple streamers across the living room ceiling and then blew up balloons, placing some on walls and light fixtures. They placed half a dozen balloons on the front light post to announce that this was where the party would be. They baked cookies and helped Sarah's mother pat ground beef into hamburgers. Then Maggie filled serving baskets with chips and nuts while Sarah cut up celery and carrot sticks.

At 5:00 Maggie dashed home to shower and dress for the party. She had promised Sarah she would be back by 6:15 to finish any last-minute preparations and help greet the first guests at 6:30. She raced out of the bathroom, just after showering. Clutching her bathrobe around her, she went straight to her room to dress for the party.

"Hi, Sugar Plum," came her father's voice from the stairs. He just stood there, smiling up at his daughter.

"Hi, Dad," said Maggie. She kept walking toward her room.

"Is that all? Just 'Hi, Dad'?"

"Oh...uh...how was your day?"

Dad skipped the last step on the stairs and joined Maggie in the hallway. "My day was fine. How about yours?" He bent down to kiss her hello.

Maggie quickly turned her head away from him. "My day was fine too, Dad." Maggie started to walk toward her room again.

Her father firmly took hold of her arm. "So, what did you do today, Princess?"

"Just hung around with Sarah."

"And...?"

"And I helped her set up for the party, that's all. Dad, I really do need to go and get ready now. I promised Sarah I would be there early."

"OK, Princess," Dad said as he released Maggie's arm. Then he added, "You know, Maggie, ever since going to visit your grandparents, we haven't spent any time alone together. I miss that. Maybe you and I can figure out something special to do together this weekend."

Maggie felt very uneasy. She did not want to be alone with her father at all. "I don't know Dad. I'm going to be pretty busy helping Sarah clean up from the party and getting ready for school. It starts on Monday, you know." Then changing the subject she said, "I really do have to get dressed now, Dad. Can we talk about this later?"

"Sure, Maggie," said her father. "Go ahead. I wouldn't want you to be late."

Maggie was all ready for the party a little after six. Her mother beamed as she walked into the kitchen. "Maggie, you look beautiful!"

Maggie's father looked over at her. "Linda, don't you think that skirt is a little short on her? Maggie, why don't you put on something else?"

"Dad, I don't want to change now. I have to go." Maggie's eyes met her mother's as she spoke.

"Jim," said Mom, "Maggie's just fine. Let her go."

"That skirt doesn't look just fine to me," said Dad. "Maggie, go upstairs and change clothes."

"But, Dad, I'll be late. Besides, this is the only thing I have that looks right for the party."

Looking from his wife to his daughter, Dad was quiet, deciding whether to push the issue with Maggie.

"Dad, please," said Maggie. "This skirt isn't that short. This is the length all the girls are wearing."

Mom looked intently at Dad. Maggie hoped this wouldn't be a fight. That was all she needed right before the party.

"Well, all right. Go ahead, Maggie. Shall I walk you up to Sarah's?" he asked.

"No, I'm fine, Dad."

"OK, then how about a kiss good-bye?"

Maggie walked over and kissed both her parents.

"What time is this party over?" her father asked.

"Oh, I don't know," Maggie said. "Mom said that I can spend the night at Sarah's. I have my stuff already packed. Katie's sleeping at Jenny's house tonight." Maggie watched her father anxiously, hoping he would not object to her plans.

He was quiet. Hearing no objections from her father, Maggie finally turned and left the room. She called over her shoulder, "Night, Mom. Night, Dad. See you in the morning."

At Sarah's house, everything looked festive with the streamers and balloons. Sarah had invited eleven classmates to her party, including Maggie. The awkwardness at the beginning of most parties quickly dwindled as the kids played charades, freeze dancing, and twenty questions. In between games there was dinner. Later in the evening Sarah turned on the tape deck and some of the kids danced. Jeremy asked Maggie to dance and even held her hand at one point during the evening. Sarah saw this and winked and smiled at Maggie.

By 9:30, everyone had gone home. Maggie helped Sarah and her parents clean up. Even after this, Sarah and Maggie were too happy and excited to go to sleep. They got into their nightgowns, crawled into bed, but lay awake talking for a long time.

"It was a great evening, don't you think?" asked Sarah.

Maggie nodded. "Yeah, it was a terrific party. I'm really glad my parents let me come."

"Well, they had to. I couldn't have a party without my best friend, could I?"

"I guess not," Maggie answered.

"Maggie," Sarah gently prodded, "I think Jeremy likes you. What do you think?"

Maggie giggled. "Oh, Sarah, I don't know."

"He asked you to dance. And I saw you guys holding hands. Sure seems as if he likes you."

"I hope you're right. Jeremy's one of the cutest boys in class. And he's really nice, too."

"Sounds like someone here likes him back."

Maggie laughed. "You know too much, Sarah Bloom. You don't miss anything, do you?"

"I try, Maggie," Sarah laughed with her friend, then she yawned. "I'm starting to get sleepy. How about you?"

"Yeah, I'm pretty tired. We should probably go to sleep."

"Fine with me," said Sarah as she burrowed under the covers. "Hey, Maggie? Thanks for all your help with the party. Good night."

Maggie snuggled down under her blankets. "Night, Sarah," she said. "See you in the morning.... Oh, Sarah?"

"Hmm?" Sarah's voice was low and groggy.

"About the party tonight. Do me a favor and don't tell my dad any details. It's just that he might make a big deal about it. OK?"

"Sure, Maggie. Whatever you say."

Maggie and Sarah woke up late the next morning. After breakfast, they dressed and walked down to Maggie's house to see if they could spend the day playing together. As they walked into the house, Maggie's father greeted them.

"Hi!" he said. "How was the party?"

"Fine, Mr. Davis. We had a good time, didn't we, Maggie?"

"Yeah," Maggie agreed. "It was fine, Dad."

"And...?" Dad kept looking at Maggie.

"And...there were a bunch of kids from school...we played some games and ate lots of food. That's about it, I guess." Maggie shrugged her shoulders. She glanced over at Sarah. "Dad, Sarah and I wanted to spend some time together today. Is that OK?"

"Fine with me, Maggie. But haven't the two of you had enough of each other yet?"

The two girls laughed. "I don't think we ever have enough of each other, Mr. Davis," said Sarah. "That's how come we're best friends."

"C'mon, Sarah," Maggie said. "Let's go up to my room and figure out what we want to take back to your house."

Once in her room, Maggie whispered to Sarah, "Thanks for not going into any details about the party."

"That's OK," said Sarah, "but I don't get it. What's the big deal about your dad knowing about the party? It's not like we did anything wrong. My folks were there the whole time."

"I know," said Maggie. "It's just that he still treats me like a little kid in some ways. I'd just rather not get into any hassles with him."

Maggie and Sarah spent the rest of the day at Sarah's house. Maggie returned home just before dinnertime. Katie was home from Jenny's house. They briefly compared notes about their days and sleep-overs. Maggie was glad to see Katie, suddenly realizing she had missed her sister. She found herself being interested in hearing about what Katie and Jenny had done. Maggie wanted to share with Katie and Mom the details of the party, but she could not risk Dad finding out. She knew what his reaction would be. Maggie reluctantly decided to keep the party to herself. ❖

Chapter Seventeen

It was cloudy and cold the next few days. Threatening rain clouds hovered above the horizon. School started again on Monday morning. Maggie felt more relaxed and alert at school than she had before vacation. She and Katie had been sharing Maggie's bedroom since returning from Pinewood. Dad had not made one of his nightly visits since the evening of her dance recital. Maggie was sleeping better at night with Katie and Nelson there for protection. She was sure this was the answer to her problem. By never allowing herself to be alone with her father, she would be able to stop the touching from ever happening again.

By mid-week, both girls had made plans for overnights with friends for Friday. Katie had been invited to sleep at Jenny's. Maggie quickly arranged to spend that same night at Sarah's house, determined not to be left alone in her own room, vulnerable to her father. Sarah had readily agreed to the plan and both girls got permission from their mothers.

On Friday, Maggie and Katie headed off to school. The plan was to return home that afternoon to pick up a change of clothes and pajamas for their overnights. As Maggie and Katie walked down the street to school, Katie told Maggie all about the plans she had made with Jenny.

"We're going to make popcorn tonight. And Jenny's dad said he'd build a fire in the fireplace. We can take blankets and pillows in there and pretend like we're camping out if we want to. Think that's a good idea, Maggie?"

"Sounds like fun."

Katie continued excitedly, "Jenny's mom is going to make spaghetti for dinner, with garlic bread, too. And we get to watch a movie if we want. What are you and Sarah going to do?"

Maggie shrugged and laughed. "I don't know yet, Katie. I guess we aren't quite as organized as you and Jenny are."

At the corner they waited for Jenny and Sarah to meet them. Soon Jenny came running up.

"Hi, Katie. I can't wait for tonight, can you?"

"Uh-uh. Me neither. We're all set, right?"

"Sure! My mom says to come over as soon after school as you like. My dad promised to build the fire right after dinner."

Just then Maggie spotted Sarah walking down the street toward them. Sarah sneezed.

"Bless you," said Maggie.

"Thanks." Sarah sniffled a bit.

"Are you OK, Sarah?"

"Yeah, I'm fine. What a worrier. One sneeze and you're worried?"

"Just don't get sick, OK?"

"You sound just like a mother, Maggie. I'm fine. Come on, we better get going so we're not late for school."

Maggie watched Sarah more closely. She looked fine, Maggie decided, even if she did keep sniffling. It's probably just the weather, Maggie thought. If Sarah was getting a cold, Maggie's parents would cancel the sleepover. But Maggie would not say a word to them about it. Even if Sarah was getting a cold, Maggie had no intention of sleeping at home alone tonight.

The morning passed quickly at school. By lunchtime, Sarah was sneezing repeatedly and her eyes looked red and runny. Just as class was being dismissed, Ms. Evans took Sarah aside. Maggie waited at the doorway for her friend. As Sarah approached, Maggie noticed that her cheeks were flushed. Before Sarah could speak, she sneezed again.

"Maggie," Ms. Evans said, "why don't you walk Sarah over to the office. She looks to me like she has a fever." Then to Sarah she said, "Ask to see the nurse when you get there. Tell her I suggested they take your temperature. If you're getting sick, you really need to be at home resting."

Maggie felt like the room was closing in on her. Everything looked out of perspective, the walls looming large in front of her while Sarah and Ms. Evans seemed to shrink in size. Maggie heard Sarah answering Ms. Evans but her voice seemed to be coming from far away.

"OK, Ms. Evans," said Sarah. As the two girls walked down the hall Maggie felt uneasy and nervous. "Sarah, you *can't* be getting sick. What about the overnight?"

"I know, Maggie. I'm sorry." Sarah's voice was low and very nasal as she spoke. "I'm feeling pretty crummy, though. Let's just go check my temperature."

"If you don't have a fever, Sarah, then we don't have to say anything to our parents about you being sick, right?"

Sarah hesitated. "I don't know, Maggie. I mean I don't think I can hide the stuffy nose and sneezing from my mother."

"But that could be from anything. Maybe from allergies or something."

Maggie and Sarah went to the school office. While Sarah talked in the back room with the nurse, Maggie sat and waited on the bench in the front office. She kept her fingers crossed, hoping this might make a difference in how things would turn out. A few minutes later Sarah came out.

"It's a hundred and one, Maggie. She said I have to call my mom." Sarah saw Maggie's expression and thought her friend was going to start crying. "Maggie, I'm sorry. We can do the overnight real soon. Maybe next weekend or something." Sarah was very apologetic.

"Oh...uh...yeah, Sarah. Don't worry about it. It's not your fault anyway." Maggie forced a small smile. Then she asked, "Do you want me to go back to class and get your stuff?"

"Thanks. That would help. I'll stay here and call my mom. And...Maggie, I'm really sorry."

"I know, Sarah. Don't worry about it."

Walking back to her classroom, Maggie tried to figure out what she was going to do. Maybe she could talk Katie and Jenny into spending the night at her house. After gathering Sarah's belongings and taking them back to the office, Maggie found Katie and Jenny in the school yard and suggested the idea to them. Katie was willing to change the plans but Jenny didn't want to sleep away from home. They would still be spending the night at Jenny's.

The rest of the afternoon Maggie tried to figure out what to do. Dad had not bothered her in three weeks. Maybe there was nothing to worry about anymore. Maybe her problems were over. After school, Katie went home to get her things and then left for Jenny's house.

That night Maggie had dinner alone with her parents. She enjoyed the quiet time together with them. After dinner, they rented a movie as a consolation prize for the cancelled overnight. Mom, Dad, and Maggie spent the evening on the couch, snuggling together, watching the movie. By 10:00, the movie was over.

Maggie stretched and yawned. "I think I'm going to head upstairs." Kissing her parents good night she added, "Thanks for helping me feel better about not sleeping at Sarah's tonight."

"I enjoyed it, Maggie," said Mom.

Her father smiled at her. "We don't get much time alone with you, Maggie. It was a nice evening."

"Good night, Mom. Good night, Dad. Nelson, c'mon, boy. Time to head upstairs."

Nelson rose slowly and followed Maggie upstairs. Maggie quickly got ready for bed and was soon under the covers with Nelson laying next to the bed. Her raggedy teddy bear, Willie, lay safely in the crook of her arm. Outside it was raining, first a few gentle drops and then a steady, heavy downpour. Maggie fell asleep quickly, listening to the rain as it hit against the window and the roof.

At some point during the night, Maggie abruptly woke up. Startled, she looked around the room. It was very dark. Small beams of light slid in from the street lamp outside, piercing the darkness. Rain still battered against the roof in short, hard sounds. Then she heard the breathing. It wasn't her own breathing. It was different than the way Nelson sounded at night, too. The breathing was followed by foot-steps. Then there was her father's voice. And his hands. Once again, the hands. Maggie tried to push away the hands but they kept coming toward her. The nightmare was happening again. Except this time she was not asleep. There did not seem to be any way to stop it. Nelson put his front paws on the bed, trying to move in close to Maggie. Her father roughly shoved him away. Maggie did not know how much time passed. Her father finally stood up. As he walked to the door, he stepped on Willie who had fallen to the ground. Before leaving the room, Dad paused for a moment in the doorway and whispered, "Good night, my Sugar Plum Princess."

Rain continued to pelt Maggie's bedroom window, accompanied now by sudden bursts of thunder and lightning. Maggie lay curled under the covers, hiding from the flashes of lightning. Cracks of thunder split the air and the persistent rain beat down. Eventually she slept.

She woke late in the morning to a damp, overcast world. As if in a daze, she remembered last night. The touching had not stopped. The only thing that had kept her safe was having Katie in the room with her at night. But Katie had not been there. No one had been there to protect her. Silently, Maggie wished for help. Why didn't Mom see what was happening and put a stop to it? Why didn't someone do something to save her? Maggie's cries for help remained deep inside, silenced by her fears and confusion.

Despite having Katie back with her the following nights, Maggie had repeated nightmares. Her dreams were filled with monsters, and always hands reaching for her, grabbing her in the darkness. After three nights of this, the dreams began to subside. Maggie started to feel a little bit safer with Katie sleeping in the room once again. But how could she keep from being left alone again? When she thought about this she felt panicky. She couldn't stop Katie from going on overnights. And Sarah was not always available.

On the fourth day after Dad's night visit, two letters came in the mail from Grandma and Grandpa. There was one letter for Katie and another one for Maggie. Maggie eagerly tore hers open. It was in Grandpa's handwriting.

Reanne S. Singer

Dear Maggie,

How's my girl? I had such a good time with you and Katie. Don't forget to use the bird book. I expect that you will know more than I do by the time we see each other this summer. Grandma and I are still planning to come for a visit at the beginning of the summer. Don't worry! I haven't forgotten about our plans for after that. I'll mention it to your parents soon. We'll work it out. Just think of all the birds that will be up here then. It's only a few months away. Write back and tell me how the party at Sarah's went and how school is going. I miss you.

Love, Grandpa

Maggie smiled to herself as she put the letter back in the envelope and carefully placed it in her top dresser drawer. Grandpa was right. Summer wasn't really that far away. Maybe Maggie could avoid the late night visits for that long. Then Grandma and Grandpa would come visit and take Maggie back with them for the summer. Maggie would just have to talk Katie into going, too. She could not leave Katie alone here with Dad. It would not be too difficult to talk her into going. Katie seemed to want to do everything that Maggie did. The trick would be convincing Mom and Dad. But Grandpa had said he would take care of that.

Once she got to Pinewood, Maggie would just refuse to come home. Somehow she would figure out a way for her and Katie to stay there, out of their father's reach. ❖

Chapter Eighteen

A month passed since Katie's overnight at Jenny's house. It was also a month since Dad had come into Maggie's room that rainy night. Maggie was satisfied that the next few months would go fine at home. Dad had not bothered her since Katie had stayed at Jenny's. Everything seemed to be all right. Then one night after dinner, Maggie stayed down in the kitchen to help Mom with the dishes. Dad went up to his study to catch up on some work. Katie cleared the table and wiped it off.

Katie came over to the sink. "Mom, if you and Maggie don't need any more help, I think I'll go get my bath over with."

"That's fine," said Mom. "I think we can handle the rest of this." Then she added, "In fact, if both of you want to head upstairs I don't mind finishing. There really isn't much left to do."

Maggie shook her head. "Why don't you go on up without me, Katie. I'll finish helping down here." Having her own bath in privacy tonight would be nice.

"OK, Maggie." Katie left the kitchen. Maggie and Mom soon heard the bathwater running upstairs.

Mom washed all the dishes within a few minutes. Maggie dried the pots and pans and wiped off the counter tops. "Thanks for all your help, Maggie," said Mom. "Do you have any homework left?"

"Just a little bit. Nothing major."

"Well, major or not, why don't you go upstairs and finish it? It's getting late, sweetie."

"All right, Mom. I will."

Walking upstairs, Maggie could see part of the hallway and the bathroom door. The door to the bathroom was partly ajar, but just for an instant. Then it closed. That's strange, thought Maggie. Katie had run the bathwater and gotten into the tub at least ten minutes ago. She wouldn't have climbed out to shut the door. Maggie reached the top of the stairs. Through the closed door she heard her father's voice.

"Here, I'll get that for you, Katie. I'm a master back washer."

Katie laughed. Then Maggie heard her say, "That's OK, Daddy. I can do it myself. I'm almost nine years old now, you know."

"Oh but Katie, I can do a much better job of that for you. Let me do it." Dad's voice sounded more insistent.

Without thinking, Maggie moved quickly to the bathroom door. With her hand on the doorknob, she could feel her heart quickly beating. She pushed the door open and forced a smile on her face.

"Hi, Katie," she said, brushing past her father. "Mind if I join you? I thought I'd get my bath out of the way before I finish my homework."

Maggie's father stood quietly watching his older daughter.

"Sure, Maggie," Katie answered. "It's fine with me."

Maggie turned to her father. "Dad, we're fine in here. I don't think we need any help."

"Well, I just thought Katie might need help washing her back."

"I can do that, Dad. We can wash each others' backs. That way you can go finish the work you wanted to get to tonight, right?"

"Sure, I guess so," said her father. Then he left the room.

"Katie," said Maggie, "I just need to go grab my nightgown and I'll be right back in."

Maggie walked to her room. She kept seeing the image of her father in the bathroom with Katie. Maggie remembered when the touching had started for her. Dad started coming into the bathroom when she was in the tub. Maggie was just a little younger than Katie was right now. There had been the back rubs, and he helped her dry off with a towel. Then the visits at night started. Maggie could not let this happen to Katie. Then she stopped short. What if Dad had already done more to Katie than just washing her back? Maggie would have to find out. This was not the first time she had come across Dad in the bathroom with Katie!

Returning to the bathroom, Maggie closed the door firmly behind her. She stood there looking at the door for a moment. She turned the lock so that no one could come in. Katie was in the tub, dunking her head under the water while she pretended to be a seal. Maggie undressed.

"Hey, Katie," said Maggie, "how about moving over or sitting up so I can climb in, too?"

Katie laughed. "I guess it's kind of hard to fit two seals in here at once, huh?"

"Is that what you were doing? Being a seal?"

"Yeah. You should try it. It's fun."

"Maybe some other time." Maggie reached for the soap floating in the water. "Katie, what did Dad want when he was in here before?"

Katie shrugged. "I don't know. Nothing much. He just said he wanted to wash my back for me. Said he's a master back washer. Why?"

Maggie tried to make her voice sound calm. "No reason. I was just wondering. Does he wash your back for you very much?"

"I don't know. Sometimes. Not a whole lot though. Most of the time you're in here with me anyway, remember?"

"Yeah, I know. But does he do other things for you?"

Katie was quiet for a moment. She looked confused. "Like what, Maggie?"

"Oh, just...touching things."

Katie looked even more perplexed. "No, not really. Just normal dad stuff. You know."

"Yeah, I know, Katie."

Maybe Dad wasn't touching Katie in the same ways that he touched Maggie. But it worried her. She just wasn't sure. Laying in bed that night, Maggie stayed awake for a long time. Finally she decided she was going to have to do something. Summer was still four months away. Now it was feeling like a long time to wait for Grandma and Grandpa to visit. What if Dad tried to touch her again during that time? What if he tried to touch Katie?

That night Maggie had another dream. A blanket of darkness

Reanne S. Singer

engulfed her, suffocating her. Maggie was hot and sweaty under the
darkness. Then she was in a cave and there was only one way in or out
of the cave. Maggie tried to escape. Suddenly hands were thrusting out
of the darkness, hands without a body or face. The hands grabbed for
her. She started to run but then she saw Katie against the rear wall of
the cave, screaming as the hands now moved toward her. Maggie was
paralyzed, not knowing whether to run out of the cave or stay and help
Katie. Waking, Maggie felt as though she could not catch her breath.
She looked around the room, assuring herself that she was not in a cave
and that no hands were coming out of the walls. Katie was safely asleep
in the other bed.

The next day was Monday. Maggie and Katie had dance class after
school. As they gathered their lunches and school books, Mom came
into the front hall and offered them a ride to school. She picked up
Sarah and Jenny at the corner, too.

The few blocks to school took only a short time. Mom pulled up in
front of the gate. "Have a good day, girls. I'll pick you up from dance
class at 5:00." She blew kisses to both daughters.

Maggie spent much of her time at school trying to decide what to
do about the night visits from Dad. She remembered the assembly at
school before Christmas: "If you are being touched in private areas,
you need to say no and tell someone." Maggie had said no but that did
not seem to stop her father. Telling someone seemed like the only
answer—someone who would believe her, who would know what to
do about the problem. The people at the assembly had suggested
telling a trusted grown-up. Maggie thought about telling Sarah, but
what could Sarah do? Maggie trusted her and Sarah might be the
easiest person to talk to about this, but deep down Maggie knew Sarah
could not make the touching stop, not without telling her parents. And
Maggie did not want to talk to Sarah's mother and father about this.

At lunchtime Mr. Bellam was out on the playground, supervising
the kids while they played. Maggie watched him. Maybe she could talk
to Mr. Bellam about what was going on at home. She had always liked
him. He would know what to do about it. Maggie started to walk across

the playground to talk to him. Kids kept running up to him to talk or to hear one of his jokes. As Maggie got closer, she slowed her pace. What if he didn't understand? What if he didn't believe her? How could she get the words out without being completely embarrassed? She stopped, then walked back to the kickball game her classmates were playing. Mr. Bellam saw her and waved and smiled. Maggie waved back and turned away.

In class that afternoon, Maggie thought about talking to Ms. Evans. There always seemed to be other students around, though. There was no way Maggie could stay after class to talk to her alone today. Sarah, Katie, and Jenny would be waiting for her to walk to dance class.

That afternoon on the way to dance class, Maggie was quiet as the others talked about the new dances they were working on. She did not pay much attention to the conversation. They turned the corner and up ahead Maggie saw the dance studio. That was it, she thought to herself. She would talk to Jill. Jill would know what to do.

Maggie quickly changed clothes. She left the dressing room and ran up the stairs. She turned toward Jill's office at the end of the hall. She would find Jill in her office and talk to her before class. Maggie knocked on her door. There was no answer. Maggie knocked again and waited. Sarah was standing at the top of the stairs now.

"Maggie," she called, "what are you doing? Jill's already in the studio. She's showing us some new stretching exercises today, remember? She said she wanted us all in there as early as possible."

Maggie's heart sank. It would be impossible to talk to Jill alone today. After class, Maggie would have to quickly change into her school clothes and meet Mom out front. There would be no time to talk. The next class would not be until the following Monday. She did not want to wait a whole week to take care of this. Maggie walked down the hall and joined Sarah.

"What's with you?" her friend asked. "You look kind of upset."

"Nothing's wrong," Maggie answered quickly. "I just had a question to ask Jill, that's all. I forgot she'd already be in the studio."

"Oh well...maybe you can talk to her during class."

"No. I don't think so, Sarah. I'll catch her another time. C'mon, we better get in there."

It took all of Maggie's effort to keep her attention focused on dance class. Her mind was filled with thoughts of home and who she could talk to. She spent the rest of the day and evening feeling like she was looking at the world through a dense fog. Voices seemed muted and people's actions seemed slower, almost like watching a movie on the wrong speed.

That night at bath time, Dad offered to help Maggie and Katie dry off. Maggie quickly declined the offer.

When he said good night to her at bedtime, Dad kissed her directly on the lips. When he said the words, "Good night, my Sugar Plum Princess," she felt her body tighten up. She wished she could make those words disappear forever. Maggie decided *tomorrow* she had to find someone to talk to. ❖

Chapter Nineteen

Tuesday, February 12th. Maggie silently repeated the date to herself. As she walked into the classroom, she decided this was the day she had to talk to someone about what was going on at home. Maggie kept to herself for most of the morning, avoiding talking with her friends. She worked on her assignments as if she were a robot, doing what was asked of her but without volunteering to answer questions in class. At recess she watched her friends play, telling them she had a stomach ache and could not join them. At lunchtime, she sat with Sarah and Emily. Pieces of their conversation sifted through to her, but she did not talk much.

In the afternoon Maggie's class studied literature. Ms. Evans had her students take turns reading aloud poetry selections they had brought to share. Then she asked them to write their own poems. Maggie sat at her desk staring down at the blue horizontal lines which ran across her paper. She could not seem to come up with any words to write down. The paper remained on her desk, blank. Ms. Evans walked around the room, offering help to any students who needed it. She approached Maggie's desk. Maggie did not notice her.

Placing her hand gently on Maggie's shoulder she said, "Maggie, it looks like you're having a rough time with the writing today. Is there a problem?"

Maggie shook her head back and forth.

"Well, then, how about trying a poem?"

Maggie remained silent, continuing to stare down at the paper.

"It's difficult sometimes to come up with an idea to write about, isn't it, Maggie?" Ms. Evans said. "You know, sometimes when I'm having that kind of problem I take a few minutes to look around and usually I can find something to write about. It could even be about something or someone in the room."

Maggie looked up at Ms. Evans. Smiling slightly, she answered, "I'll try that. I'm sorry. I guess I was just thinking about some other things."

"Well, you could write about those things if you like, Maggie."

"No, that's OK," Maggie quickly replied. "I'll try your idea of looking around the room. I mean, I think that will help me write the poem."

"That's fine, Maggie. If you need any more help just raise your hand and I'll come over." Ms. Evans continued walking around the room, reading students' poems and offering suggestions.

Maggie wrote a poem about a picture on the wall that one of the students had drawn. Fifteen minutes later, Ms. Evans walked over to the light switch and turned the lights in the room off for a moment. That was the signal for everyone to quiet down and listen to her directions. She turned the lights back on.

"Class, it's almost time to go home. I'd like you to make sure your names are on your papers. Pass them to the front of the rows and I'll collect them. If you're not done with the poem, don't worry about it. We'll have time another day to finish them. Then we'll spend some time illustrating them, drawing a picture that tells about the poem. Right now it's time to clean up and get ready to go home."

A few minutes later the bell rang. School was over for the day. Quiet and order gave way to the commotion of students gathering up their belongings and talking excitedly about the day and plans for the afternoon. Maggie sat at her desk, not moving.

Sarah, Emily, and Lisa were at the door when Sarah turned and called, "Maggie, we're going to be out on the playground for a little while. Do you want to come with us?"

Maggie looked over at her friend. "I don't know, Sarah. I'll be out in a little bit. I need to take care of something."

"Well, we'll be out by the monkey bars. Will you be long?"

"I don't know. Don't bother waiting for me. Oh, and if you see Katie, just tell her to walk home with you if I'm late."

Sarah walked back across the room to where Maggie was sitting. In a softer voice she said, "Maggie, did Ms. Evans tell you to stay after school? Are you in trouble?"

"No, it's nothing like that. I'll be out in awhile. I just need to talk to Ms. Evans about something. I'll see you later."

Sarah walked back to the doorway. She turned and then waved and smiled at Maggie. Joining Emily and Lisa, she walked out to the playground with them.

Ms. Evans was at her desk going through papers and organizing the next day's lessons. Maggie approached Ms. Evans' desk, walking between the rows of desks lined up in the classroom. Noises from the school yard floated in through the open windows. The noises made a stifling sound in Maggie's head. As suddenly as the sounds arose, they retreated into a dark quiet. All Maggie heard now was the insistent scratching of Ms. Evans' pen against papers on her desk. Maggie was halfway across the room when Ms. Evans looked up.

"Maggie, all the children have gone. Did you forget something?"

Maggie stopped where she was, silent, just shaking her head no. She stared hard at the linoleum floor. Her focus moved to the tennis shoes she was wearing. Over and over Maggie concentrated on the pattern of pink and blue stripes on her shoes. She counted the number of air holes forming a semicircle along the side of each shoe.

Looking more intently at Maggie, Ms. Evans saw that she was upset. "Can I help you with something, Maggie?"

Maggie looked up at Ms. Evans. Slowly she walked toward her teacher. She stopped a few feet from Ms. Evans. Maggie opened her mouth to speak. The words caught in her throat. Maggie felt like she was choking. She rubbed one hand against the other, then grabbed a finger with the other hand and pulled on it. She looked away from Ms. Evans and back down to her shoes. There were eight tiny air holes on the outside rim of her right shoe. Another eight on the outside of the left shoe. Three pink stripes alternated with three blue ones, and they formed arches extending from one side of the shoe to the other, reaching over the toe of the shoe.

Maggie heard Ms. Evan's voice again, gentle but persistent. "Maggie, whatever the trouble is, you can tell me. I'll try to help."

Maggie did not answer but continued staring down at her shoes. Then Maggie flashed on Katie's face. In her mind she saw Katie playing and laughing. She saw Dad hugging Katie and Dad going into the bathroom when Katie was in the tub. She remembered her dream and saw Katie trapped in the cave. Then the words came tumbling out. They were slow at first, but then they came like an avalanche gaining speed and force.

"I...it's about home...I mean, well it's my...dad and me." Maggie was gasping for air, trying to get the words out and having difficulty talking and breathing at the same time. Her heart was racing; she could feel the blood pounding in her head. "We...I don't think it's what happens to other girls. I think we're...different and that it isn't OK. I don't know if you can help but I don't know who to tell." The tears came now. Maggie reached up and tried to dry her cheek with her hand. The tears continued. She brought her hand back down to her side, drying it on her sweatshirt.

Ms. Evans came closer and put her arm around Maggie's shoulder. Maggie was trembling. Ms. Evans brought Maggie over to a chair and with reassuring pressure on her shoulder sat Maggie down. Ms. Evans pulled her own chair around to face Maggie.

"Maggie, I want you to take a deep breath and try to slow down. Then I want you to tell me what's going on."

With great effort Maggie sucked in some air. Shaking more, she continued, "It's just that..." The shaking increased. Once again Maggie was having to gulp air into her lungs. "He kisses me good night but...he doesn't kiss right. He...I can't explain it." Maggie ended in frustration, not knowing how to find the words to make Ms. Evans understand.

In a calm, reassuring voice Ms. Evans said, "Maggie, you're doing fine. Just tell me in any way you can."

"He touches me. He comes into my room at night and he...he touches me. I try to tell him no but he says that this is how people show they love each other." There were more swallows of air. Then Maggie said, "I don't want him to...but he won't stop. I can't make him stop!"

Ms. Evans was quiet for a moment. Then she asked, "Maggie, what do you mean he touches you? Can you tell me what kind of touching you're talking about?"

Maggie stared at her lap, getting lost in the pattern of lavender flowers on her pants. With her index finger she traced over and over again the stalks and leaves of the flowers.

"Maggie," Ms. Evans prodded, "did you hear me? Would you tell me more about what goes on at home?"

Reluctantly Maggie raised her head and looked at Ms. Evans. She studied the wrinkles lining her teacher's face. Ms. Evans' soft gray eyes looked at her intently and helped Maggie focus on what Ms. Evans was saying.

Maggie's voice was now a whisper. She spoke slowly, with long pauses. "Dad touches me...he moves...he takes the covers off me...when I'm in bed." Then her voice rapidly gained in volume and she spoke hurriedly. "His hands...he puts them wherever he wants and he kisses me." Now she was yelling. Her fists pounded on the desk next to her. "I hate him. I want him to stop it. He won't. I tell him but he won't even listen to me!" Maggie's fists continued to pound on the desk.

Ms. Evans reached over and firmly put her hands on top of Maggie's fists, stopping the pounding and holding Maggie's hands against the cold surface of the desk. Maggie brought air painfully into her lungs; each breath was an immense effort. She realized her face was wet. Tears were streaming down her cheeks. She laid her head down on Ms. Evans' hands as they held her own hands. She cried and cried, one sob after another, until she was afraid she would never stop. After a minute, Ms. Evans pulled one of her hands free and gently stroked Maggie's hair.

Maggie could hear her saying, "I'm glad you told me, Maggie. It will be all right. You'll be OK."

Maggie tried to speak through the tears. "But, how? I don't know what to do." Maggie sobbed harder, unable to talk any further.

"Maggie, it will be all right. When you calm down a little bit we'll walk up to the office together and..."

Maggie looked up and shook her head from side to side. "No, I can't. You don't understand."

"Maggie, we have to. That's the way we can take care of this. I have to make a phone call to some special people who can help you with this. They will talk to you and help so that this doesn't have to happen again to you."

"But how can I tell anyone else about this? I thought that you could make him stop."

"I can help, Maggie, by letting the right people know what's going on. They will be able to make your father stop. Come on, Maggie. Let's take this one step at a time." ❖

Chapter Twenty

It was September, seven months since Ms. Evans had reported Maggie's father for child molestation, seven months since Maggie had told the secret. A new school year had started two weeks ago. Maggie was in the seventh grade now. She had one more year at Lark Street School and then she would go to eighth grade at Lincoln School.

Sarah and Maggie sat out on the grass near the swings. "You should have seen the wildflowers this year, Sarah. They were incredible. They covered the hillsides up at my grandparents' house. Yellow, pink, orange, lavender, blue!"

"Sounds beautiful, Maggie. Did you go bird-watching with your grandfather, too?"

"Of course," Maggie laughed. "You think I could make a trip up there and not go bird-watching?"

Sarah shook her head. "I guess not. Knowing your grandfather he probably had you out searching for birds by 6:00 every morning."

"Not quite that early. But we did spend lots of time hiking around, carrying our Audubon books with us. It was fun."

"Well, I'm glad you didn't stay forever like you had talked about," said Sarah.

Maggie was quiet. Taking in a slow, deep breath she said, "Yeah, I guess by the time summer came I didn't really need to go away for a long time, did I?"

Maggie and Sarah looked steadily into each other's eyes for a moment. Maggie was glad she had a friend like Sarah to talk with. She had been afraid to tell Sarah about the molestation and explain to her why her father no longer lived at home with the rest of the family. But it would have been even more difficult to lie to Sarah. Maggie didn't want to lie to anyone anymore. She hated the secrets.

"You know, Maggie," said Sarah, "I don't think I've told you this before, but I'm really proud of you. I think you're probably the bravest kid I know, maybe even the bravest person I know!"

Maggie felt her cheeks redden. She did not say anything.

Sarah continued, "I mean...well, I don't know if I could have gone to Ms. Evans and told her all about the touching the way you did. I just think it took a lot of guts to do that."

"Thanks," said Maggie. "It *was* scary. I just got to a point where I had to tell somebody. I couldn't let the same thing happen to Katie that happened to me. And I guess I couldn't let it keep happening to me either."

"I'm glad it's stopped, Maggie. Have you talked to your dad lately?"

"A little bit," Maggie answered quietly. "It's still real weird though. He's sad and I'm still real angry at him. Dr. Andrews—you know, the therapist I'm going to—says it will get easier. She says that someday we'll be able to talk about what happened and maybe work it through. It's just so hard, though. I talk about it at my therapy sessions and Katie and Mom have to go to some, too."

"Do your grandparents know?" asked Sarah.

"Yeah. They were great. They didn't push me, but they were there to talk with whenever I wanted. Mom called them right after I talked to Ms. Evans. That's why they came down for such a long visit in the early spring instead of waiting until summer. When Katie and I were up there this summer, my grandpa told me this story. He talked about the storms they get up in the mountains. They come on so strongly that there is no way to escape them. It's like the storms are in control of everything—with the rain and the thunder and lightning. They're really powerful. But the storms always end. Then the next day it's beautiful and everything is all clean. It's like the storm changes it all. He said there's a special moment that's called 'the storm's crossing.' That's when the storm is still there. You can see the rain and lightning and hear the thunder, but the storm has started to blow away. The storm's not nearly as strong then and you know it'll be over soon."

"What did your grandfather mean by all that?"

"He said my family had gone through its own storm, with the molestation. I've been changed by it, but I have strength inside. Plus I have many people who love me and care about me. He told me he knew it was still hard for me but that eventually I would be OK."

Maggie and Sarah sat quietly for a few minutes. Maggie looked at the students passing by. In the corner of the school yard was a girl about Maggie's age, sitting by herself. All week long, Maggie had noticed her, sitting alone during lunchtime. She looked sad and preoccupied much of the time. Maggie thought this girl looked a lot like she must have appeared to Sarah and her other friends last year. Maggie did not know much about this girl, though. She was new to the school and seemed to be shy and quiet. It must be uncomfortable, Maggie thought, coming to a new school and not knowing anybody. But the other kids had tried to be friendly. Maggie had seen them approach this new girl and try to get her to join in.

Emily and Lisa walked across the playground toward Sarah and Maggie. "Hi, you guys," Emily called.

Maggie and Sarah waved and smiled at their friends.

"Race you to the swings," said Lisa.

"You're on," said Maggie. "Just let me get up, otherwise it won't be a fair race."

"OK. You have till the count of three, Maggie. Then the race officially starts. Sarah, you call it."

Maggie quickly got up, laughing.

Sarah called out loudly, "On your mark, get set, GO!"

Maggie and Lisa were off running toward the swings. Maggie reached them first.

"You win," Lisa yelled happily. "Let's see how high we can swing."

Maggie was already seated on the swing, pumping her legs back and forth, using her whole body to propel herself. She still loved swinging, though she was almost thirteen. The air was warm. Sunlight shimmered through the branches of a nearby tree. This feels good, Maggie thought. The bright sun made her back and head feel toasty warm. Maggie continued swinging, back and forth, back and forth, higher and higher. With each forward motion she stretched her legs out straight, reaching with her toes for the blue sky. This must be what a bird feels like when it's flying, she thought—soaring high above the ground, feeling the wind and the sun all mixed together.

"I think it's a tie," yelled Lisa.

"Isn't this great?" Maggie called back. Maggie stopped moving her legs, allowing the swing to slow down. The slowing motion was calming, soothing.

Maggie's thoughts turned to her therapy session last week with Dr. Andrews. She had been going to see her therapist now for six months. Dr. Andrews spent most of her time talking with kids who had some sort of problem. She said she worked with many kids like Maggie who had been abused or molested. She also worked with families, trying to help them change and understand their problems. Maggie liked going there to talk and play the games Dr. Andrews had around her office. Sometimes they drew pictures together or made things out of clay. Every Wednesday night, Maggie also went to something Dr. Andrews called a support group. It was a time when a few kids got together to talk about what was going on with them. Maggie remembered hearing some of the kids in the support group talk about molestation and abuse. They believed they were the only ones in the world who went through those kinds of things. Maggie was surprised to discover how similar their experiences and reactions were to hers. And she was relieved when she realized by talking with the kids in her group that the touching was not her fault.

"Lisa," said Maggie, "do you know anything about that kid sitting over there?"

Lisa shrugged. "I don't know much about her. I think her name is Michelle. I don't think she talks much to anybody. She always looks worried or upset."

"It must be hard coming to a new school, don't you think?"

"Yeah, I guess so. She sure isn't going to make friends just sitting by herself, though."

As the arc of the swing got smaller, Maggie jumped off into the sand below. She stood up and brushed off her jeans.

Turning to Lisa she said, "I'll be back in a few minutes. I want to go do something." Maggie walked across the yard to where Michelle was sitting. Maggie did not know what she was going to say. She just knew she wanted to try to talk to this girl. As Maggie got closer, Michelle looked up and glanced shyly at Maggie. There was something about this girl that touched Maggie. The expression on her face, the way she held her body, sitting off by herself; it all reminded Maggie of herself seven months ago.

"Hi," she said. "I'm Maggie Davis."

"Hi," came a soft reply.

Maggie sat down on the grass next to the girl. The voices of children playing carried over to where the two girls sat. After a moment of awkward silence, Maggie said, "It's kind of strange coming to a brand new school, I bet."

Michelle nodded her head.

"It's not so bad around here, though," said Maggie, "There are lots of nice kids." Maggie looked across the yard. Sarah and Emily had joined Lisa over on the swings. Sarah waved to Maggie, motioning for her to come over.

"Want to go swing?" asked Maggie.

"No, I don't think so," murmured Michelle.

"C'mon," Maggie prodded. "It's fun."

Michelle got up and cautiously followed Maggie over to the swings. Maggie's friends watched curiously as the new girl approached. There were two unoccupied swings.

"C'mon, Michelle," Maggie said as she motioned to one of the empty swings. Maggie climbed onto the other.

"Ready, set, GO," yelled Lisa. "I'm going to win the race this time, Maggie."

Maggie laughed. Soon she was soaring again. The motion of the swing sent her hair flying behind her. The ground was far beneath her. Maggie and her friends laughed together as they reached for the sky.

❖ ❖ ❖

Reanne S. Singer is both an author and a clinically trained licensed psychologist. She works extensively with children, adolescents, and families. Much of her work is with survivors of abuse and molestation.

Dr. Singer has been practicing psychology for thirteen years. She maintains a private practice and does agency work in substance abuse and the treatment of juvenile offenders. She also supervises and trains counseling interns in individual and family therapy.

The Storm's Crossing is Dr. Singer's first book for young adults. She has written two other novels for children and preadolescents. She is currently working on an adult novel. She lives in Ventura, California with her two children. ❖